# The Heart's Desire

## S. R. Burks

A NOCTURNA PRESS BOOK

ISBN-13 978-1-944673-01-7 (paperback)
ISBN-13:978-1-944673-00-0 (e-book)

ISBN-10:1-944673-01-6 (paperback)
ISBN-10:1-944673-00-8 (e-book)

Nocturna Press
Independence, Missouri
www.NocturnaPress.com

Published and Designed by Nocturna Press

Library of Congress Control Number: 2016949783

# Chapter 1

He stormed out of the house, slamming the door behind him. The force shook the foundation. He fumbled for the keys in his pocket, his feet hitting the pavement hard. He made his way to the gold SUV, but he was so enraged that he could hardly steady the remote to unlock it. He finally got in and within seconds he'd backed out of the drive and sped away.

"Damned woman! I can't take it anymore!" he growled. As he peeled down the road that would lead him far from the estate, he broke every traffic law that had ever been written. The evening played over and over in his mind and soon he was racing down a country road to who-knows-where.

After a while, he didn't know where he was or even how long he'd been driving. Suddenly, without warning, a deer leaped in front of the vehicle. He swerved to miss it and slammed on the brakes, but he lost control. The car slid from side to side then veered toward a tree. Pain shot through his body and everything went black.

Dale Banner lived in the woods, some distance from town. She was a quiet person and tried to keep a quiet life. Although she didn't socialize often, people in town knew her to be a strong and warm-hearted person. She was also quite pretty with delicate brown skin and a sparkling smile that could charm most anyone. But she didn't put much stock into the opinions of the townsfolk. She trusted her dogs more than anyone and preferred solitude rather than socializing.

She took nightly walks enjoying the quiet, the starry sky, and the way the moon shined down like a beacon. But one night she decided to forego her usual routine and stay in. She felt a minor cold coming on.

During dinner, Duke and Banshee cocked their ears and began to bark. Dale stood from the table and walked to her front door. She watched and listened for whatever had riled them up, but observed nothing.

"Whatever it was, it's gone now," she said as the dogs peered through the screen door. But just as Dale turned away, she was shocked to hear some type of explosion in the distance. She quickly went out to the porch and looked in the direction of the sound.

Duke and Banshee were barking like crazy. She was concerned, but knew the sheriff and one of his deputies made regular rounds about that time and it was probably safer to let them handle it. She closed the screen door and returned to her meal. But Duke and Banshee weren't as sure as their master. They stayed at the door as if to protect her whether she warranted it or not.

Nothing else strange was heard, so Dale went to bed early. She wanted to sleep off that cold. After a while, she was in sweet utopia when again she heard the sound of dogs barking. It drew her from her comfortable place, and plunged her into consciousness. Her eyes flew open. Her ears tuned in with what was going on around her. Duke and Banshee began to growl.

She jumped out of bed and grabbed her shotgun. She had learned to trust those two long ago. She peeked through the window and surveyed the area.

"Whoever or whatever got you two in an uproar can certainly be taken care of," she said. She opened the front door and unlatched the screen. "Go!" she commanded. They immediately obeyed, taking off like hunters in pursuit.

Dale ran behind the dogs, trying to keep up with their fast pace. She broke through the brush before her and the dogs had stopped in their tracks. They were sniffing at something she couldn't clearly see. As she came upon what they had found, she saw it was a man.

Dale wasn't sure if he was alive or not. She poked him a few times with the barrel of her gun without any response. She bent down to check his neck for a pulse. He had one, but it was very faint. She looked around to see if there was some type of evidence as to how he got all the way out there and began to wonder if he was involved in the incident earlier. For now, however, he was in terrible shape. She knew she had to get him to the cabin.

Duke and Banshee guarded the injured man while Dale retrieved a sling to pull him onto. When she tried to move him, she realized the size of him. He began to moan and groan and was slowly exiting the darkness he had fallen into. But his energy had been spent by the struggle to seek out help.

When Dale got him inside, she tried to call the sheriff's station but there was no answer. It was a small town, and she suspected everyone was tending to that explosion, or whatever it was. She also knew she couldn't leave him to go for help and she shouldn't try to move him again. "No matter what happened," she said to herself, "I'm sure Craig and Seth are taking care of it."

Morning came quickly, and Dale was up with the dawn. She prepared breakfast for two this time. She'd be sure the stranger was all right and then question him about what happened.

In the spare bedroom, the sun's rays beamed across the man's face, causing him to stir from his sleep. He shifted his body slightly, then shouted in pain. Dale froze when she heard him. He was awake.

She went to the room to check on him. He didn't notice her at first, but then his eyes shot anxiously to the woman at his side.

"Lie still," said Dale. She pulled the covers back to check the bandage she'd wrapped around his ribs the night before. The stranger looked over the woman tending to him. She was attractive, he thought. She had a pretty face and deep hazel eyes. But his mind was riddled with questions.

"Who are you?" he asked. "And where am I?"

"My name is Dale," she replied with a smile. "And you're in my cabin."

He looked around the room. It certainly wasn't familiar to him. "Do I live here with you?" he asked, searching her eyes for something familiar.

Dale stopped abruptly and stared into his eyes. "No, you don't," she replied. "Don't you remember? I found you out cold in the woods and brought you here. I think you were in some type of accident." She could see that he was very confused.

"No, I don't remember," he said, and began to rub his head.

Dale went into the bathroom and emerged with a medicine bottle. She opened it, took his hand into hers, and put two pills in it. He immediately popped them into his mouth. She handed him the glass of water that was next to the bed.

"Thank you," he said. "I don't remember anything."

Then Dale thought of something. She went over to his clothes and began to search them for a wallet. Maybe there was an ID or at least something to jog his memory. He watched, wondering what she was doing. She stopped when she found something and stared at it for a long time.

"What is it?" he asked.

"It just says 'Jackson'," she replied. "I can't make out the last name, but it seems to start with an M." She handed him the piece of paper, thinking maybe he would recognize it.

"Jackson, huh, maybe my name. It looks like some kind of cleaner's slip." He tossed the paper aside.

Dale was surprised that no one from the sheriff's office had come through and mentioned yesterday's incident. "I'm going to call the Sheriff and let him know you're here," said Dale. "Maybe someone has reported you missing." She turned to leave the room, and as she did a panic suddenly struck him.

"Wait," he pleaded. "Do you really have to do that?"

Dale could sense something was eating away in him. She paused to study his face. Something was playing in his mind. "Do you remember something?" She came over to the bed.

"No, it's just a strange feeling," he said. He laid back and covered his eyes with his arm.

She sighed softly. She had the feeling he was running from something. But did he know it? "Well, the sheriff usually makes rounds this way every day anyway. He's probably on his way here this minute. And you haven't eaten anything. I'll get you some breakfast and we'll take it from there," she said with a smile. "You take it easy."

While Dale prepared some breakfast, she asked herself all sorts of questions about where the stranger might have come from and whether he'd really lost his memory. Somehow she felt she could trust him, but her mind strayed to thoughts of his long brown hair, his immense height, and his neatly-trimmed moustache and goatee. He had breathtaking green eyes and his mouth was made for kissing. It had been a long time since she had those thoughts.

*He walked into the huge house. It had been a long and tiring day. All he wanted was a hot bath, a beer, and shot of whiskey to soothe his nerves. He saw the mail was still lying on the floor beneath the drop. He guessed he'd come home first. He went into his office and threw the letters on his desk. He would deal with them later. He walked up the stairs and down the hall to his room. He paused for a moment, thinking he heard a noise coming from inside....*

Jackson woke from his dream and could smell the food that Dale had cooked. His eyes parted as he felt a tray being placed over his legs. He looked at the beautiful smile that greeted him.

"Here, let me help you sit up," said Dale. "Just move slowly." She placed an arm under his, and told him to scoot upwards by pushing his feet. He moaned and groaned his way up to a sitting position.

"Thank you, ma'am," he said, looking at the plate of food before him. He was indeed hungry.

Dale gave him a look that he didn't see. "Jackson," she said. "Whatever you do, please don't call me ma'am. I hate it with a passion. Dale will do. Now eat. You need to get your strength back."

When she turned to leave, he asked her to stay. She looked at him first and then to the ground before sitting in the chair at his bedside. She felt something growing inside her. It had been a long time since she'd been so close to a man. Not since—Dale stopped herself and let her mind go blank. She wasn't ready to relive that time in her life.

"I was wondering if we couldn't hold off on telling anyone that I'm here?"

Dale just stared and wondered what he was hiding or suppressing. "I told you before, Jackson, the sheriff will stop by and if you were involved in that crash or explosion I heard, he'll be asking questions. I've never lied to him before." She stood and walked away from him.

"I'm not asking you to lie, Dale."

She snapped her head around to face him. It was the way he said her name. It brought memories back to her mind. She took a deep breath. "Okay," she said. "But just until you get on your feet and we can figure out who you are. And I'll have to think of who you will be to me."

Dale felt that he was beginning to remember something and wasn't ready to share it with her. Or maybe he was running from something—*or someone*.

## Chapter 2

Dale was just finishing up with cleaning the dishes, when she heard Duke and Banshee barking. She went to the window and saw the sheriff's car approaching. She wiped her hands with the dish towel and went to the door. She paused for a moment trying to get her story straight. She glanced over to where Jackson was sleeping, then opened the door and went out onto her porch to greet her old friend.

"Hey, Dale!" he said, getting out of his car and stopping for a moment to pat the dogs.

"Hiya, Craig," said Dale. "What brings you out here?" she asked innocently.

The sheriff came up to her and seemed to be searching for something. "While you were on your

walk last night, did you see or hear anything unusual?"
he asked, taking his hat off and wiping his head with a
handkerchief.

"I didn't take my walk last night," Dale replied.
"I was feeling kind of under the weather." she said

The sheriff looked at her strangely. He'd never
known Dale to let anything to keep her from making
her nightly walk.

"Really?" he asked with a tone of disbelief.

Dale noticed. "Why Craig, you have a sense
disbelief in your voice." She sounded a little hurt.
"Anyway, what's so important that you needed me to
have taken my walk last night?"

The sheriff paused, realizing he had hit a nerve.
Then thought better knowing Dale wouldn't lie to
him. "Well, there was a car accident near the road
here. Thought maybe you heard or saw something
that might be useful." He turned to look at the two
dogs playing in the yard.

Dale thought she should be at least a little
helpful. It wouldn't look right if she said she hadn't
heard or seen anything at all. Especially since Duke
and Banshee had the keenest ears in the country.
They would've made a racket.

"You know, Duke and Banshee were barking like mad dogs last night. I thought I was going to have to give you a call. But I figured it was nothing. Later, I heard a loud noise, but I knew you'd take care of it, whatever it was."

"Well, thanks for your help," said the sheriff. "You take care now."

He began to walk to his car. Then Dale added more to further sway suspicion. "Was anyone hurt?" she asked, coming partly off her porch. The sheriff stopped and turned to stare at her.

"Don't know. Didn't find anyone. You be careful. We don't yet know exactly what happened."

He opened his car door and got in. Dale waved as he backed away. She smiled to herself, pleased with how it went. She thought she had done a very good job. She slowly backed onto the porch, making sure the sheriff was gone, then went inside and backed against the cabin door. She took a deep cleansing breath.

"Never lied to him before, huh?"

The voice was so near it startled her. She clasped her chest as if to keep her heart from jumping out of it. Jackson was standing by the window. He had heard the dogs barking and heard her go out the door. He got out of bed to see what was going on.

"What are you doing up?" she asked. "You scared the devil out of me." She sat down in a chair, trying to calm her breathing. He walked over to her and sat on the couch, staring at her.

"I heard the dogs barking, and didn't know what was going on," he explained. "You really haven't ever lied to him have you?" He realized she was anxious because of what she had done and not so much that he had startled her.

"I told you so," said Dale. "I just hope I can regain his trust if he ever finds out that I lied." There was some sadness in her voice. He could see this was really bothering her.

"Look, you don't know me, and you don't owe me either," said Jackson. "I'll go up to the road and flag someone down. Or, if you can take me near the town, I'll tell them I've lost my memory and try to get help." He didn't want to see her so upset. She had been so good to him, and he owed her.

"No, Jackson, we made a pact," she said. "And we'll see it through. Besides it's already in motion. Can't turn back now," She rested her head back onto the chair.

"Only if you're sure," he said. "How much sleep did you get last night anyway?" He moved closer and could see that she was a bit out of it.

That's when she noticed he was in his boxers. "Oh!" she cried and turned her head.

Jackson smiled. Modest too, he thought. "I'm sorry, I'll go put my clothes on." He said, and started to walk away.

"Wait," Dale said. "You can't wear those clothes. They're ripped up. I have some things that might fit you."

It was a lot different last night when she'd taken his clothes off; he was knocked out. But now he stood fully awake, and very much a man.

She went into a room and moved around a bit. Jackson stood against the door frame in the room where he'd slept and listened to her moving around. She soon emerged with a stack of clothes and handed them to him.

"These belonged to my late husband," she said. "I hope you don't mind wearing them."

Jackson saw how sad she'd become. He'd known it wasn't possible for a woman like her to have been without someone. This explained things. He'd thought a man would have to be a fool to have left a woman like her, or he would have to have died. He was saddened to know it was the latter. He wouldn't ask her to talk about it now.

"I don't mind at all, Dale. Thank you," he said as he took them into his arms.

Dale left him and went out to the porch to sit in a rocking chair. As she rocked back and forth, her mind drifted to a happier time. She thought of what once had been, and what could have been, but never will be...

"Sandy, hon, I'm sorry to ask you to stay after closing but Dave had a family emergency." Dale walked up to her assistant with apologetic eyes. The girl moaned softly, but knew any protest was futile. There always had to be at least two to count, along with a security guard.

"All right!" she agreed. "Let me call my husband and tell him it's going to be a late night." She reached for the phone on her desk, to make her call. He would have to pick the kids up from school, fix dinner, help with homework... suddenly she smiled. This was going to work out great after all.

Dale leaned on the desk silently. She didn't want to be the cause of a family discord, but she was the manager of the bank and sometimes had to make tough decisions. "How did he take it?" Dale asked. "Sandy?"

Sandy was about to answer but her eyes moved passed Dale and were growing large at the sight before her. Dale's eyebrows crinkled. Then she turned to see what had Sandy's undivided attention.

He stood about six feet, six inches. His hair was short and blonde. His eyes were the clearest blue and could make any woman melt. He was certainly a tall drink of water. Dale clutched her chest, holding her heart in. He was coming their way.

"Wow..." was all Sandy could say.

The man approached Dale and her eyes traveled up his body to those beautiful eyes that were now locked on hers.

When Thad walked into the bank, inquiring about opening a business account, Dale was pointed out to him. She was a cutie, he thought. Eyeing her smooth brown skin, 'hot chocolate' came to his mind. And he loved chocolate. He measured her to be about five feet three inches. She had a voluptuous figure with nice wide hips. She was just what the doctor ordered. But when she turned to face him, he was immediately drawn into her mesmerizing hazel eyes. He was hooked.

"Hi there. I'm told I should speak with Dale Sayers," he said. His voice was deep and soft and had just a hint of a southern accent.

Dale pulled herself together. "Hello. I'm Dale. What can I do for you?" She leaned against Sandy's desk, where her friend was hiding her face in her hands holding back a chuckle. Dale was more than her boss. She was like a sister. And she was hoping from Dale's reaction, something might come from this.

"Well, for starters, I'm new in town and would like to open a business account."

Dale hung on his every word. His smile was hypnotizing. "Okay Mr—"

"Banner," he replied. "Thaddeus Banner. You can call me Thad. I hate that formal stuff."

She felt she could just die and go to heaven. Sandy peeked around to look at Dale's face. Yep, he had her. She smiled and sat back down.

Dale led him to her desk where they completed the transaction. Dale found it hard to concentrate. He never took his eyes from her. He just smiled and sometimes seemed distracted, causing her to repeat what she had said.

"Okay, Thad. You're all set. Good luck with your business. I hope you enjoy our little town," she said with an honest grin.

Thad sat back in his chair and began to contemplate. His expression was intense.

"Is there anything else I can help you with?" Dale asked.

"Yes," he replied. "Would you have dinner with me tonight?"

Dale was taken aback. "I don't know if that's a good idea." She stood and walked around to the back of her chair.

Thad stood also, being the gentlemen that he was. "Oh, I see. Husband," he said.

"No! No husband or anything like that. It's just that you're a customer and all." Dale tried to convince herself too. Because deep down something told her this was it.

"I'm new here and don't know my way around town," he said, feigning sadness.

"Uh, Dale—Dave is on his way back," said Sandy. "Why don't you show the good man around town? We wouldn't want our brand new customer to get lost, now would we?" Sandy grinned from cheek to cheek.

"She does make a point," Thad said to Dale. "Thank you Sandy."

Dale balled a fist and made her some promises.

"Anytime, Thaddeus. Anytime." Sandy turned and bounced away.

Dale had sucked in her lips and Thad took note of it. When she's nervous she bites her lips, he thought. "Well, is it a date?" he asked.

"Not a date," said Dale. "But I wouldn't want you to get lost, so... I'll be finished here about seven o'clock. I'll see you then."

She extended her hand to complete the deal. He took it gently and brought it up to his lips for a kiss.

His lips are so soft, Dale noticed. He released her hand and walked away. Dale watched his every move and had to catch her breath....

"What?" A gentle hand had touched Dale's shoulder, bringing her back to the present and to the pain of her loss.

"You were so far away I didn't want to call out and startle you," Jackson said softly. He could see something serious was on her mind.

"Oh, okay. Thanks," she said, trying to gather her thoughts and hide her emotions.

Jackson took a seat on the porch and watched the dogs play. "Do you want to talk about it?" he asked.

"No, it'll be all right" said Dale.

Jackson already knew when to press and when not to. He leaned against the pole and sat quietly. Dale continued to rock, freeing her mind. The sun was high and moving to the west, preparing for its afternoon descent.

## Chapter 3

Jackson sat on the steps of the cabin. It was his first time outdoors since Dale found him. He listened to the creaking of the chair while Dale was rocking. He knew something was on her mind, and that she wasn't ready to discuss it with him. And he respected that. After all, they were still strangers to each other. But even more, he was a stranger to himself.

His eyes roamed over the cabin. The porch was long and had two chairs and a table at one end, and the chair Dale sat in was at the other. To Jackson's left was a large carport and to the right a beautiful lake with small pier. An old boat lay ashore. Ducks and swans swam about.

In front of him was an open area with a dusty road that wound through the trees. The cabin was surrounded by woods and hidden from the road. The sun hung high, it was late afternoon. Dale stopped rocking and turned to Jackson. "I'm going to fix you something to eat. You're still building your strength. Are you going to stay out here?" she asked.

Jackson stood to his full height. "I think I might go down to the lake and take it in. It's beautiful," he said.

"Yes. Thad built and landscaped the property the way he knew I always wanted. Just you be careful, you're only beginning to heal."

She left him staring after her as she reentered the cabin. Jackson shook his head, sensing there was a great love between her and her late husband.

Jackson took his time moving down the two steps and began his walk to the lake. Unknown to him, Dale watched through the window. Something in her was stirring. It was the way he walked... so much like her Thad... maybe too much. She left the window and began to prepare lunch. She tried to shake what was growing in her heart.

Jackson stood on the pier watching the ducks and swans glide across the water. He found it humorous that the swan, which was the picture of grace in the water, now waddled clumsily up the bank. It was like him, he thought. He felt awkward, not knowing who he was. He felt out of his element much like the swan seemed on dry land.

Was he married? Did he have children? What did he do for a living? These questions plagued him, yet something in his heart told him that he wanted to forget.

Arriving back at the cabin, he saw Dale setting plates and utensils on the small table for two. He stopped and stood under a shade tree, watching her move in and out of the house. Was she the kind of woman he would fall in love with? What was his type? He didn't know what it was in the past, but as he said before, a man would be a fool to leave a good woman like that behind.

Dale saw him standing under the tree. "Jackson, food is ready," she said sweetly.

He started for the cabin, taking careful steps, but he cringed from the pain around his ribs. Dale moved to help him, but he politely waved her away.

"I'm okay," he insisted. "It hurts like hell, but I can't let it set in."

"You should go back to bed after this," said Dale. "You were just in an accident last night. And nearly killed," she reminded him, as he waited for her to take a seat.

Then Dale realized why he was still standing. She sat down and he followed. He's such a gentleman, she said to herself.

"I have to go into town tomorrow," said Dale. "Will you be okay until I get back?"

"Do whatever you need to," said Jackson. "I'll be all right," he assured her.

"While I'm there, I'll see what information the sheriff has dug up. Are you sure you don't want me to let him know you're here? Someone could be looking for you... a wife maybe?" Dale looked down at her food, feeling a twinge in her heart. What if he does have a wife? She'd be worried about him. Dale would be. Who wouldn't?

"No Dale, please. I don't know why, but I have a feeling something more than an accident caused me to wreck last night." His eyes stared into hers, pleading.

Dale felt herself inhale and hold her breath. "Okay, Jackson, we'll do it your way," she promised.

As they sat together, Jackson took notice of Dale's every movement. Somehow, being with her made him feel as if a hole in his heart was being filled for the first time.

Jackson lay in bed, napping, and Dale peeked in on him. He'd done too much his first day. She closed the door and went to sit by the fireplace. She watched the flames dance. This soothed her just as much as her walk. Duke and Banshee were getting antsy. The sun would be setting soon.

"You two relax," she said to the dogs. "We'll be going in a while. Remember we have a guest." She leaned back in her chair, thinking how good it felt to have someone besides herself in the house. Well, someone with whom she could hold a two-way conversation. "But how long, Jackson?" she whispered to herself. She knew his memory would come back sooner or later.

*Jackson walked into the huge house. It had been a long and tiring day. All he wanted was a hot bath, a beer, and shot of whiskey to soothe his nerves. He saw the mail was still lying on the floor beneath the drop. He guessed he'd come home first. He went into his office and threw the letters on his desk. He would deal with them later. He walked up the stairs and down the hall to his room. He paused for a moment, thinking he heard a noise. He went up to the closed door and listened. Yes, there was a noise coming from the other side. He placed his hand on the doorknob and slowly turned it. The noise grew louder as the door opened. It was dark. He brushed his hand up the wall, searching for the light switch. Finally, he clicked it on....*

"No!" yelled Jackson, sitting up in bed. Pain instantly shocked his body and he grabbed his side. Soon, the door swung open and Dale came ran running in.

"What is it, Jackson?" she asked. She grabbed the pain pills and poured fresh water into his glass.

"Thank you," was all he said. After taking the medicine he lied back down.

Dale was curious, but didn't press him, for she wasn't the only one holding back.

"I'm going to let you rest," she said. The dogs and I are going for a walk. Supper is going now. Will you want to eat, later?" Part of her hoped they could eat together under the moonlight.

"I think I'll pass, if that's all right," said Jackson.

She smiled and nodded her head, leaving the room. She closed the door behind her and leaned against it. He's not yours to claim, she reminded herself. She went to the room she'd shared with Thad and looked over his things in the closet. They gave her comfort. She needed that now.

Dale, you need to get a hold of yourself, she thought. You know nothing of this man. He's not Thad! The love you shared with him was a once in a lifetime. Nothing could ever match that. Then she broke down and began to cry.

Jackson felt bad after Dale left his room. He wanted to tell her he would eat with her after all. Still in pain, he got out of bed and went in search of her. He smelled the delicious food that was cooking, but saw she wasn't there. He saw Duke and Banshee, lying by the door, so he knew she hadn't yet gone. Then he heard a voice from her room. He went over to it and was going to knock when he heard her crying. He slowly backed away. He had hurt her badly. He went back to his room and sat on the bed, knowing he had repaid her kindness rudely. He would have to figure a way to correct this.

After a while, he heard her come out of her room. He left the bed and walked over to the door, watching her go into the kitchen and then exit it shortly afterward. She glanced into his room and gave him a quick smile.

"We're going for our usual walk. Try to take it easy while we're gone." She said and opened the cabin door. Duke and Banshee rushed out of the door, barking at the creatures that had emerged for the night. Jackson thought of an idea to make things better.

Dale walked up the winding road away from the house. Her life had been simple since the death of her husband. She hadn't let anyone in since then. Her routine was the same. But now, there was a disruption. She stuck her hands in her jean pockets and walked down the roadside. A first for her. Usually she would stick to the wooded area, but for some reason she wanted to take this path. Maybe because this was the same path that led Jackson to her.

She looked up at the sky and began to count the twinkling stars. This was a quiet road. Yet this was probably where Jackson had his accident. She still wondered how he had escaped with just a few bruised ribs and a jolted memory. He was very strong. And for this reason, she knew his memory would come back to him.

Soon, Dale decided she stayed out long enough. She started back to the cabin when she heard movement behind her.

"Hey, Dale! I see you're out on your nightly walk."

She spun around and was face to face with the deputy.

"Hi, Matt!" she replied. "Yeah, you know me. Same ole, same ole!"

He patted the dogs as they greeted him. "I heard you didn't have your walk last night. Somethin' about you not feeling good. I'm glad you're better now... you takin' your walk and all."

"Yeah, feeling a little better," said Dale. "Didn't want to miss another night." She answered carefully, trying to recall exactly what she'd told the sheriff.

"Yeah. You sure did miss the big accident, though. If you'd have had been out here, you would've seen it," he insisted. He sounded quite excited that something happened in their town.

"Yeah, I probably would have," Dale agreed. "Well, I guess I'd better be going back now. Don't want to overdo it. You know, with being sick yesterday and all."

"Sure. Oh and Dale, I've got something to tell you," he began.

Dale planted her feet and stared hard at him and he knew why.

"Now Matt, you know how I am about gossip," she warned.

He looked down at the ground and began sliding his foot left to right in the dirt.

"I know. But this is official business, not gossip!" He looked up in time to see Dale cross her arms.

"Which makes it even worse!" she reminded.

He took a deep breath. "Okay Dale! Good night!"

"Goodnight, Matt. Take care."

Matt watched as Dale walked away. She always made him feel like a kid. Hell, he was twenty-eight years old, and only a few years younger than her. But there was something mature about her. That's why he never acted on his impulse to ask her out. He feared she would shoot him down, much like she'd just done.

As she walked, Dale's mind wandered back to another time, to another man who had touched her heart...

Dale rode impatiently next to her new husband as they cruised out of town in a limousine. She watched in great anticipation. Thad had been building their dream home and wouldn't allow her near it until after their wedding. Their first night in their new home would mark the beginning of their new life.

The night had come. They had become husband and wife and their friends and family were left at the reception to party. It was a very electrifying night. The stars and moon were bright. All forces were working in their favor.

"Oh, Thad! I'm dying from the suspense. Please tell me how far are we have to go!"

He smiled widely. "Nope. I'm not telling you a thing. Just hold your horses." He pulled her to his side. She leaned into his chest looking straight ahead.

"I can't wait till we get there," she said. "This is driving me-" At that moment the car turned off into the woods. "Where in the world are we going?" Moments later, her question was answered. "Oh, Thad!" Tears swelled in her eyes.

The driver exited the car and opened the door for them. Thad stepped out first and offered his hand to his new wife. She was too awestruck to move.

"Dale, baby! You have to leave this car if you want me to carry you across the threshold. You know, make it all official."

She gazed up into his eyes. Never in her life had she felt so much love for one person as she did at this moment.

"Oh yes, my darling husband. Let's do make it official." She placed her hand into his and exited the car. He sent the driver on his way, thanking him. Dale looked over to see the moonlight dancing on the lake.

"Thaddeus Banner! You took everything I told you I wanted in a dream home and made it come true."

"I did it for you," he replied with a smile. Then he lifted her into his arms and carried her into their new home....

"Damn, damn, damn!" Dale cried. Those were the happiest of times. And yet, they were the most heart-wrenching. She fell to the ground, squeezing some dirt between her fingers, gripping anything she could. And she broke down and cried. Duke and Banshee lied next to her, whining.

# Chapter 4

Dale had wiped her tears and sat poised against a tree. As she gathered herself, she looked at the moon and the twinkling stars. Everything seemed strange to her. The atmosphere warned of something approaching, as if after tonight, nothing would ever be the same. She rose to her feet and dusted herself off.

She approached the back of the cabin and the dogs ran ahead. She was deep in thought as she came around to the front. And when she went up the steps she paused. "Oh my," she said.

Lighted candles were at each corner of the porch. The table was beautifully set with a single red rose and a candle in the center. she was speechless. "Oh, my," she repeated.

"This is all for you," said Jackson as he approached. "It's my way of saying thank you, for everything."

Jackson decided to give her something she probably hadn't had in a while... some tender loving care. He'd found a nice tablecloth and candles, and picked a rose from the garden. He wanted to make it nice and serene. It was a beautiful night. There were a lot of forces working together. Both good and bad. But right now, he felt the forces were in favor of them. All they could do was follow their lead.

Dale went to freshen up and when she returned she was just as amazed as before. She looked deep into Jackson's caring eyes. He placed his hand gently on her back and guided her to her seat.

"Tonight, sweet lady, I will wait on you hand and foot," said Jackson.

Dale could hardly contain herself. No one had been this nice to her, since Thad.

Jackson had taken what Dale had made and served it on a platter and other beautiful dishes. After everything was in place, he sat across from Dale.

"Thank you, Jackson," said Dale. "This is really sweet of you," she said, her voice breaking.

He gazed into her eyes. "No, Dale, thank you. You took a big chance on a stranger. And you protected me. I will always remember your kindness."

"This is amazing," she said. "How did you know how to set everything up like this? It's so... elegant."

Jackson had just taken a bite when a familiar feeling coursed through him. "I don't know," he said. "It just seemed to come to me as I started to put it together."

"Well, it's very nice. Thank you again," said Dale. She took a sip of wine and felt the warmth of it flow through her body. She hadn't taken a drink in years. She hated drinking alone.

"Well, the night is not over yet," Jackson said with a smile. "I have a bigger surprise waiting for you after you've finished eating."

Dale's demeanor suddenly changed. She hoped he wasn't expecting anything to happen between them.

He could almost read her mind from her expression. "Dale, you're a very sweet lady. One a man would be proud to call his own. And I would never do anything to disrespect you, ever." He leaned back in his chair stared off into the darkness.

Dale felt like a fool. "Please accept my apology," she said. "It's just been a long day. I didn't mean-" She couldn't finish.

"Yes, you did," he corrected. "Why wouldn't you? You don't know me from a hole in the ground."

Dale's eyes shot up to meet his. They stared at each other for a few moments and then broke out in laughter. The night and the wine were finally taking effect.

When Jackson and Dale finished eating, he cleared the table and told Dale not to move a muscle, and that he would take care of everything. He went inside, leaving her to her thoughts and her glass of wine. She was sitting on the steps when he returned.

"Sweet lady, follow me please," said Jackson, extending a hand. She laid her hand in his and watched him close his around hers.

He made her close her eyes and she giggled as he led her through the house. She suspected where he was leading her, but she humored him. She heard the door squeak open and warmth hit her face. There was a wonderful aroma of peach in the air.

"Open," he said finally.

Dale opened her eyes and gasped. A candle-lit bath. "Jackson!" She turned to look at him. He had a brilliant smile.

"I've laid out everything you need," he said. "So all you have to do is enjoy it. I'm going to turn in now. You go and relax."

As Jackson turned to leave, Dale caught his arm with her hand. "Jackson, wait!"

He looked down at her hand on his arm and then his eyes went to hers. His whole body went numb. What he saw in her eyes mirrored what was in his heart. A burning desire.

"Yes?" he replied, his voice barely above a whisper. He turned fully around to face her. Her hand slowly moved from his arm. For a moment in time, they stood there silently gazing into the other's eyes. The pounding of their hearts and bated breaths were the only sounds.

"I wanted to thank you for all of this," Dale managed to say. "It's been a long time since–"

She stopped and turned away, not wanting him to see the tears in her eyes. He placed his hands on either side of her shoulders turning her to face him. "I know," he said. "Since Thad. He seems to have been a good man. I'm glad you had someone like him in your life. You deserve the very best."

"Thank you for your kind words," said Dale.

"No thank you," said Jackson. "You took a chance and helped me. So this is the least I could do." His hands were still on her shoulders and his heart was aching. He knew he had to leave before he did something he would regret.

He let his hands fall to his side and smiled at her. Then he attempted to make his escape once again, but again, she stopped him. This time, she moved into him and lifted her hand to stroke his face. He closed his eyes, savoring her touch against his skin.

She let her hand trail down his face coming to rest on his chin. He could feel her moving even closer. And her face was nearing his. He bent his knee to meet her, only stopping due to a slight twinge of pain. His arm went around her waist. He looked into her eyes one more time assuring himself that what they were saying was true. Then he captured her lips with his own and kissed her with all that was within him. Her body relaxed against him returning his burning kiss.

Jackson pulled her tight. Their kiss was intense. Her arms circled his neck, as she pulled herself up to receive more of him, relaxing her body into his. The pain, once prominent in his ribs, had subsided. Only passion was left behind. He knew that Thad had been a lucky man to have her in his life. And now he had this one opportunity to feel the love this beautiful woman possessed.

He wanted her. And when she moaned with desire, it sent vibrations through his body. She felt her fires igniting. She wanted him, she needed him. She began whimpering for more than the kiss, feeling his manhood pressing against her pelvis.

Then something in the back of his head sent off a warning. Don't do this, it said. It's wrong. He pulled away and stared into her passion-filled eyes.

Feeling his arms release her, she was confused.

"I can't do this, Dale. Not to you," he said.

"I don't understand," said Dale. "Did I do something wrong?"

"No, you did everything right," he replied.

"You're confusing me," said Dale. "I thought—" She paused, running her hands over her head. Her eyes wandered the room, coming to rest on a flickering candle.

"You thought this is what I wanted?" said Jackson. "Oh, baby, you don't know how much I do. But I can't. I can't do this to you."

When Dale looked into his eyes she knew what he meant. "But I want you to," she told him. "I don't care about tomorrow. We have tonight, Jackson."

"No. I couldn't live with myself, knowing I made love to you only to turn around and find out who I really am. Where would that leave us? I can't give you anything Dale. I can't promise you anything."

He knew this was hurting her, because it damned sure was killing him. He wanted to throw inhibitions aside, scoop her up in his arms, and take her far away, so no one could ever find them.

He left and closed the door, and listened as she began to cry. He felt like a heel, but she would thank him someday. Just not today. He walked away from the door and went into his room. He would leave tomorrow. That would be the kind thing to do.

He sat on the side of the bed, pondering how he would leave. He laid across the bed thinking of something that had run through his mind. His memory may be resurfacing. While he was with her, he felt as if he hadn't been loved in a long time. And that there was someone in his life, but not like Dale.

Dale was someone who any man would be privileged to have in his life.

He realized lying there that he was exhausted. The last two days had taken their toll on him, physically, mentally, and emotionally. He soon drifted off to sleep, Dale prominent in his mind. He whispered her name.

Dale sat on the edge of her bed. She contemplated whether she should throw caution to the wind and take what she wanted, or just allow him this time to figure who he was. He was being honorable and she should respect that. What if she was only feeling lust and not love? This man has been through a trauma and is still going through it now. She laid back on her bed and slid between the sheets. It wasn't long after she rested her head that the sandman came to visit. She was out like a light.

## Chapter 5

When Jackson awoke the next morning, he could hear birds chirping outside the window. He stretched his muscles and began to open his eyes. When they acclimated to the sunlight he remembered last night. "Dale!" he shouted.

He searched for her to no avail. He then opened the front door to a warm lovely day. Duke and Banshee were sleeping under an old oak tree. Then he knew Dale wasn't around or they would have been with her. He took one last sweep over the grounds, then went back into the cabin. He wondered where she had gotten off to so early and if she'd already gone to town.

Dale drove into town, a place she really hated. But she needed supplies so it had to be done. She pulled up in front of the grocery store. It was one of the older establishments, and even though newer supermarkets had moved into town, she still preferred the smaller place.

"Hey, Hank!" She called to the man behind the counter, as she came through the screen doors.

"Hey, Dale," he replied, leaning over the counter and reading a newspaper. "How've you been?"

"Just great," she said and removed a piece of paper from her shirt pocket.

"You seem chipper this morning," said Hank. "I heard you were under the weather. Don't seem that way now." He straightened up and watched as she moved through the store. She paused, knowing where this was going.

"Hank! I never figured you for a gossip!" She teased, knowing he was one of the biggest in town.

"Oh no! Just concerned that's all. I'm glad to see you doin' okay!" He cleared his throat and went back to reading.

Dale sighed a breath of relief. She began picking up things she needed and bringing them over to the counter. He would give her a quick glance over the paper each time. He wanted badly to question her on the gossip going around town. There was a rumor that she knew something about the accident and wasn't telling.

The little bell above the screen doors signaled that someone had entered the store. It was the sheriff.

He had watched Dale drive in and go to the store. He wanted to ask her a few more questions. He still got the feeling something wasn't right and she would have the answers. When Dale saw him, she felt her heart fall into her stomach. Her day had just gone from joy to dread.

"Hey there, Hank," said the sheriff as he sauntered up to the counter and leaned on it with one arm. He pulled out a pipe and stuck it in his mouth. He didn't smoke anymore, but when pressed he would bring it out as a security.

"Hi there, Craig. What can I do for ya'?"

"Nothing right now," said the sheriff. "But maybe later."

Hank and Craig were old friends. And along with Dale, Hank was one of the few people who called him by his first name. Craig was watching Dale and she pretended not to notice.

"Hey, Dale! See your feeling much better," he said. "It was a little sudden don't you think?"

Dale exhaled, turned to face him. He just couldn't leave well enough alone. "Yes, it was," she replied. "But it might have been something I ate, that's all."

He stood straight up, his eyes never leaving her. "But I thought it was a cold or somethin', you did have the sniffles," he reminded her.

Dale worried this was going to get bad.

"Dale, what's wrong?" he asked, noticing a change in her expression.

She became desperate, she couldn't let Jackson down. Not now, not ever. "Sheriff, I'm insulted. I have lived here how long? Nearly eight years. And in that time, have I ever given you cause to doubt anything I have done or said?" She spoke in a calm, but angry voice. She walked up to him a glared.

The sheriff put the pipe back in his pocket and swallowed hard. He'd really upset her, now she was calling him sheriff rather than Craig. No, she hadn't ever given him a reason to doubt her, but this time, his gut told him better. "No you haven't Dale. But that don't mean nuthin'. Sometimes people can get in situations that make them do things that they'll regret.

I'm your friend, Dale. And I don't want to see that happen to you."

Dale backed away, seeing in his eyes something she hadn't noticed before. She never knew. She was speechless for a moment. Then her emotions overruled. "I told you everything I know. Stop badgering me," she spat.

"Hank, have my stuff sent out to me." She slammed her shopping list on the counter and stormed out of the store.

She fumbled to get her keys into the lock. Once she had got the door open. She jumped in and tried to gather herself before hitting the road. She looked up to see Craig standing in the doorway, staring at her. He was hurt, but mostly concerned. This wasn't the Dale he knew.

When she back out of the space, she narrowly missed hitting an oncoming car; the driver honked to warn her. She waited a moment, catching her breath. Then seeing that the coast was clear, backed up and sped away. Craig came all the way out, watching her as she rushed out of town.

"What's up with her?" asked Hank, who'd come outside.

"I don't know, Hank, but I aim to find out," said Craig. Hank scratched his head and went back into his store.

When Craig got back to his office, he took off the cowboy hat he always wore outside. He hung it on the rack and took a seat behind his desk.

Matt was sitting at his own desk reading a magazine. He was mildly obsessed with the high society life of the rich and famous. "Was that Dale tearing out of here?" he asked, never taking his eyes from the page.

"Yeah, it was," Craig replied. He put his feet up and leaned back. She wasn't acting her usual self and that bothered him. He didn't want to think the worst, but he had been a lawman for many years, his instincts were always on point. Something or someone had her riled up.

"I saw her last night walking down the road, near to where that accident happened," Matt told him.

Craig looked over at him. "Really?"

"Yep," Matt replied.

Craig looked straight ahead.

"She didn't seem all that sick to me," Matt continued.

"She didn't seem so sick to me neither," said Craig. "Did we ever get a hit on that partial license plate?" he asked. Matt looked up for the first time.

"Not yet," he said.

"Well, this could be something for the Feds," he told him. "We're dealing with a missing person," he finished. He left his seat and went to look out the window.

Matt had a very vivid imagination and it was starting to get to him. "What if this person is out there with Dale?" he suggested. "And what if he's threatening her?"

He came from behind his desk. Craig slightly turned his head to the side. "Then why didn't she make her escape when she came to town?" said Craig.

"Maybe he threatened to hurt her dogs. You know how much she loves them," said Matt.

Craig thought about it. Matt was right. Banshee and Duke were like her children. They were gifts to her from Thaddeus, her late husband and his dear friend. "Maybe I should pay her a visit and keep my eyes open while I'm there." He retrieved his hat from the rack and stopped at the door. "Send the plate into the FBI, and let them know this could be a missing person case. Explain we didn't find the body and see what they want to do next."

As Craig went out to his truck, Matt rushed out with one more question. "What if Dale is keeping him there of her free will?"

Craig stopped in his tracks. "If that's true, there's nothing much anyone can do. But if it's anything else, there's plenty I will do," he warned. Then he got in the truck and drove away. He had made a promise to Thaddeus. If anything ever happened to him, he would take care of Dale. And he aimed to keep that promise.

*Chapter 6*

Dale drove down the road fighting back the tears streaming down her face. Why didn't she see this before? She had no idea. She had been so caught up in her loss of Thaddeus, she had tuned out everything and everyone.

"Damn you, Craig! Why didn't you tell me? Why?" She'd understood that he would check up on her because he and Thad were such close friends. "But why didn't I see this before?" she berated herself. Then her mind began to speak to her. You wouldn't have seen it if last night hadn't happened. Jackson made you remember what it looked like for someone to gaze at you with love. And how it felt to be loved.

"Well, it didn't matter what Craig felt about me. I couldn't see it because I didn't have the same feelings for him. But Jackson was different."

Jackson! She needed to get back to him quickly. She'd just told Hank to have her groceries delivered, and even worse, she knew her behavior will have made Craig even more suspicious. She would have to hide Jackson until things calmed down.

She pulled off the highway and onto the winding road to the cabin. As she rounded the bend, she immediately saw a beautiful site. It was Jackson out in the open, playing with Duke and Banshee. She stopped the car and jumped out.

"Where did you go?" Jackson asked.

"I'm sorry, I had to go into town for some things. Remember I told you?" She walked passed him and took a seat on the porch. "I didn't want to wake you. You looked so out of it."

"Oh yeah, I remember you telling me last night," he said. "I guess it slipped my mind," he looked at her, a half smile on his face. She knew why it was there.

"It might not be safe for you here," she told him.

"Why?" he asked.

"My friend the sheriff cornered me again. I didn't react very well," she said.

"Oh."

"I flew off the handle and accused him of badgering me," Dale admitted. She stood and began to pace.

Jackson stood silently. This was his doing, not hers. He had asked her to betray the trust she had built in her community, by harboring him. He could be anyone–a murderer, robber, or anyone that the police could be after.

"I'm sorry, Dale." He walked up behind her and gently grasped her arms, and turned her to face him. "I had no right to put you in this position," he said.

"No Jackson, I had a choice," she said. "And I chose to help you. Just like I'm choosing to help you now. Get in the car."

He stared as she rushed to toward it. Soon she was in and beckoning him to come. He took a couple of strides with his long legs and was inside.

"Where are we going?" he asked.

"Somewhere no one has ever known about but Thad and me," she said as she drove away.

Sometime later, Craig arrived at Dale's home. He slowly exited his truck and peered around. He was curious to why Dale's car was nowhere to be found. She'd had ample time to get there. "So where are you, Dale?" he whispered to himself.

Duke and Banshee greeted him, walking alongside him as he made his way toward the cabin. Even though they were friends, he wouldn't enter without her permission, unless he had a search warrant. And that's something he didn't want to obtain just yet. He wanted to count on their friendship to let him look around freely.

He took a seat on the porch, pulled out his pipe, and faked smoking it. He looked around for tell-tale signs of what was going on with Dale. He felt once inside he could pick up something. But until then, he would relax and wait for her return.

Dale led Jackson deeper into the woods and came to a spot along the river that was secluded from prying eyes. They entered a wall of trees and continued down a dirt pathway, much like the one near her cabin. They came into a clearing. There was a small cottage surround by a white picket fence, a garden in front on either side of the walkway.

She parked under a carport and left the vehicle. Jackson followed. He looked around. This place was different than the rugged cabin. Even though secluded, this house was like one from the city.

"Thad thought it would be a good idea to have a home away from home," she explained. "Visit the city without visiting it," she said. "He did a lot of traveling. And whenever he took vacations he didn't want to be surrounded by people. So we would come here," she said with a smile.

"What about you Dale?" asked Jackson.

"What do you mean?" She was confused.

"You have shut yourself off from the world completely except for when you go to town," he said. "And how often is that?"

"I haven't needed to be around other people," she told him. "I had my Thaddeus." She turned away from him.

"I know," said Jackson. "And I understand what a great love you two had. But he was always interacting with others while you stayed isolated out there at the cabin."

Dales eyes darkened. "I was never isolated," she said. "I had a choice then, as I do now."

"Don't get me wrong," said Jackson. "I'm not accusing you or Thad of anything. But not knowing who I am is making me feel as if I'm shut off. And

61

seeing you living like this makes feel the same for you."

She stared into his eyes. Her own wet with tears. What he was saying was true. Before Thad she lived a busy life as a bank manager and had friends. It was routine to have girls' nights or go on spontaneous trips. At no fault of Thad's, she had allowed him to become her entire life. And she paid the price for that after he died. She had lost touch with her dear friend Sandy, and didn't have the energy to reprise the friendship.

"I'd better get back," said Dale. "I wouldn't be surprised if Craig has already been there."

Jackson grabbed her arm tenderly. "I never meant to hurt you, Dale. "Not last night, and not now."

She couldn't look at him. Last night was still imprinted in her mind. His touch and kiss lingered even now. He was slowly filling that space that her husband once occupied.

"I know Jackson," she said softly. "You were right to stop us before we made a mistake." She freed herself from his hold and left him. He watched her get in the car and drive away. He had much to think about, and this would be a good place to start.

Craig had fallen asleep in that chair on the porch. His legs were outstretched, his hat over his face. But he awoke when Dale arrived.

"How long have you been here?" she asked.

"Long enough," he answered. "I thought you would've been here by now."

"After your questioning me in front Hank, of all people, I decided to take a long drive." She hadn't lied.

"I apologize, Dale. I shouldn't have done that. But I'm concerned about you. Since that night, you have been acting a little strange."

She turned away from him to catch her breath. "I have been a little off," she said. "Someone had an accident near my home, and now, you think I'm hiding them out. I'm concerned that if you don't know where they are, then they could be anywhere around here."

"Then move to town and stay in one of the motels," said Craig. "At least until we find the person, or persons, who belong to that vehicle. We have no idea if they're dangerous or not."

"And what would I do with Duke and Banshee?" Dale asked staring directly into his eyes. Once again, there it was... she quickly turned her head.

"I can take them to my place," he offered.

"No, I can't ask that of you," she said. "We'll be fine."

"Why not?" he asked. "Damn it, Dale. Thad asked me to watch out for you. But you make it so damned hard." He rose to his feet, pulled out his pipe, and shoved it in his mouth.

"I know he did," said Dale. "And you have done that very well, Craig. But this time, you don't have to worry. I've got a shotgun and two alarm systems. Anyone who comes near here will get filled with buck shot."

Their little conversation put Craig's mind at ease. If she was involved with whoever was in that accident, she gave an award-worthy performance.

He didn't need to see what was inside. This was out of his hands. He said his goodbyes and left her rocking on her porch. She watched him disappear from her sight. She felt bad for lying to him, but until Jackson regained his memory she had to keep him safe.

*Chapter 7*

Dale sat in her chair, rocking back and forth, contemplating everything Jackson said. She couldn't be angry with him. She'd made the choice to withdraw into herself, he didn't have an option. And she guessed that's why he questioned why Thad would allow her do so when he was alive. Again, Dale began to reflect on that time in her life...

It had been three years since Thaddeus and Dale Banner were married. It was the happiest time of her life. For over a year, his business was booming. Dale had left work to begin a family. But after many attempts, they were unsuccessful.

"Dale!" Thad called, as he entered the cabin.

Dale came out of the kitchen drying her hands on her apron. "Hi, Baby. You look so tired." She kissed him hello, and he pulled her closer and deepened the kiss. Then he stared into her eyes and thought how he loved her more than life itself.

"Go get cleaned up," she said with a smile. "I've got something to tell you after dinner." She was beaming and he looked at her suspiciously, but she refused to give anything away.

Thaddeus was anxious the entire meal, wondering what she had in store for him. But on their after-dinner walk, she finally told him the news.

"What!" he exclaimed, swooping her into his arms. "A baby? We're going to be parents!" He was absolutely ecstatic. "Oh wait! You should be sitting down... resting. And I'll take off work to take care of you. Don't you worry about a thing." He led her back to the cabin and helped her sit on the couch. He fussed over her the rest of the night. Dale knew she was in for a long several months.

The couple gave birth to a daughter, named Channon. She was their greatest joy. But one night, while Thaddeus was away on business, the baby developed a fever. She was admitted to the hospital. When Thaddeus arrived, he ran through the halls in search of his wife and child. But when he finally saw Dale, he knew that the worst had happened. The world had come crashing down around them....

Months had passed since Dale hid Jackson away at her secret cottage. And she had evidently satisfied Craig's curiosity. He didn't come around as much, and whenever she went to town he never pressed her. Dale would occasionally ask if there were any leads on the car crash. Craig felt whoever was in the crash had moved on. It wasn't his problem anymore, and as long as Dale was safe, that's all that mattered to him.

"Jackson," Dale called, entering the house.

He came down the hall from the bedroom to greet her. He'd adjusted to living there, especially since Dale made it a habit to spend as much time as she could with him.

"Hello," he said.

"Three months, can you believe it?" she said, stocking the cabinets and refrigerator.

No, he couldn't believe so much time had passed. It seemed to go by quickly, but he'd become quite comfortable. It felt like home.

The only possible reminder of his other life was the recurring dream of walking through a house and hearing noises at the bedroom door. He never discussed the dreams with Dale. He figured he had put her through enough.

"I never gave time much thought," he said to Dale as he helped put the groceries away.

"You never gave it much thought?" asked Dale. "What if you're married or have children? What if you have parents or siblings who are searching for you?" She continued putting things away as she awaited his response.

Jackson wasn't sure why, but deep inside he didn't think that was the case. Something had him driving like mad down that road, and that's the main thing that has been weighing on his mind. "Don't you think if that was the case, someone would be searching for me?" he asked. "If someone reported me missing, wouldn't Craig have found out by now?"

Dale began to bite at her lip; something Jackson had witnessed on numerous occasions. It meant she was deep in thought.

"Maybe they have made some sort of report, and because you're hiding out, no one can identify you," she suggested. "And maybe the car was so badly damaged, it wasn't possible to trace it to you or match its description to a report."

Jackson poured a glass of water and leaned against the counter. "What are you suggesting Dale?" he asked. "After all this time, would you like me to just show up in town like I don't know who I am or where I was?"

She smiled at the irony of it all. "But that's the truth, isn't it?" she asked.

His eyes went blank, actually it wasn't a lie. "Well, to be honest, I don't think I want to know about some life I was running from," he said. "But do you believe if I thought there were children involved that I would run?" he turned away disappointedly and began to start dinner.

Dale could see this was upsetting, not knowing if he had abandoned children, and hoping that was not the case. She slowly came up behind him to comfort him, but he didn't see her. When he turned around with a pot of sauce, they bumped into each other and the splatter got them both.

"Oh!" Dale cried. "I'm so sorry!"

"It's okay," he said with a laugh.

"I better go change," said Dale.

"Me too," he said. "I'll have dinner ready by the time you get back. You are coming back—aren't you?"

"I'm not leaving," she said. "I have clothes here." She walked down the hall and entered the first room.

He was aware of this. He had searched the house thoroughly getting to know Thaddeus. What Jackson didn't know is that Dale had made plans for that night. Every time she had to leave it was harder and harder to do so. She had fallen deeply in love with Jackson. And if he left tomorrow she didn't want any regrets of what might have been. She knew his memory would return and send him back to his other life. And when that day did arrive, she wanted to know that, for at least one moment in time, he was hers.

Jackson was cleaned up and changed before Dale. He had the table set beautifully and dinner was ready. He turned around in time to see Dale coming down the hallway and in view. His heart nearly jumped from his chest. He had never seen her like this. Her hair was down and flowing just below her shoulders. She was wearing a long gown with a matching robe. She looked radiant. The night they almost made love had never been revisited, but this night would be different. Their eyes met, and for a moment in time that night came back to them.

Dale turned briefly away. "I couldn't find anything else to wear, so I decided this would do."

Jackson knew then that she hadn't just come for dinner. She had plenty of clothes in the next room. But it didn't matter, because he felt they had waited long enough for what he knew they both wanted.

"You look very lovely," he said.

She smiled, glad that he approved.

"Won't you sit down?" he said, pulling out her chair. "Dinner is ready."

She did as he asked. They chatted only a little throughout dinner, as both were thinking about what would come after.

When dinner was over and put away. The two sat in front of the fireplace. Winter was nearing and there was a chill in the air. Dale rubbed her arms and Jackson took notice. He pulled the blanket from the sofa and draped it over her shoulders.

"Is that better?" he asked.

"Yes," she replied. "Much better."

She looked deeply into his eyes and he knew then that he couldn't resist the longing he saw in them. She wanted to be loved, and she wanted the love that only he could give to her.

He leaned over and covered her mouth with his own. She eagerly welcomed him as his tongue slid deep inside. His body was alive before his mind could catch up. Suddenly, he broke away and looked at her. "My darling Dale," he said softly. "Are you sure this is what you want?" He knew the answer. The feeling was bigger than both of them. But he wanted to hear it from her lips.

"More than anything in my life," she replied. "If we make love and I lose you tomorrow, I will have no regrets. But if we don't, I certainly will."

He didn't say another word. He lifted her into his arms and carried her to the bedroom he had called his own for the last few months. He placed her on the bed and laid next to her. He found her mouth once again and kissed her with a greater passion than before. She let out a moan. This night would begin the rest of their lives.

His tongue danced with hers. Her taste was satisfying; her warmth was comforting. His hands cradled her face as he continued to kiss her.

Dale could hardly contain herself. There was a burning fire within her that had been ignited months ago. It needed to be sated and she knew that only

Jackson could do this. His tongue was arousing sensations that had laid dormant for years.

Jackson lifted his head. Brushing his mouth against hers, he stared into her beautiful pleading eyes. How could he not give to her what she wanted—and even more so, what he craved. He pulled off her robe and helped her out of her gown. He felt a surge of energy course through him when he finally gazed upon her hungry body. Her eyes were fixed on him. Her heart and breath were racing as she anticipated his next move.

Jackson caressed her body, explored her erotic spots, and caused her to shift and writhe and moan. The return of his powerful kiss exhilarated her. His mouth left her lips and moved down to her neck. This intensified the sensations already coursing through her body. She grabbed the front of his shirt and ripped it open breaking the buttons. He moved to his knees, his eyes locked on hers. He took the shirt off and threw it away, then proceeded to unlatch his belt. By this time, Dale's hands came to assist. She unzipped his pants and he removed them. She wanted him even more than before.

Jackson came down to her, their bare skin meeting each other for the very first time. She let out a small gasp, realizing there was no turning back. Any reservations she may have had, were null and void.

His mouth returned to her lips for a tender kiss and then made its descent down her body, preparing her for what was to come. This time her response was more vocal. He enjoyed the noise she was making; it increased his desire for her.

As Dale began to writhe even more, he knew he was doing it just right and how badly she needed it. Eyes wide open, she surrendered her body, mind, and soul. She clutched the sheets. She'd forgotten this feeling—one she'd denied herself for so many years. Her heart pounded hard against her chest. Her body was alive at last with emotions she wasn't able to control.

The time had come. Jackson moved over Dale like a warm blanket. Foreplay had come to an end, the joining of two hearts and spirits had begun. He gazed into her eyes, his own eyes darkened with hunger for this beautiful woman. "I love you, Dale," he said.

Tears filled her eyes. Hearing those four words validated that their lovemaking was not simply physical, but emotional. "And I love you, Jackson," said Dale. She wrapped her arms around his neck and pulled him to down to her covering his mouth with her own and kissing him deeply. Within moments, they were joined completely.

Outside in the dark of night, the moonlight shined on the small cottage. The creatures of the night were oblivious to two people consummating their love for one another. Their bodies entwined, only the shades of their skin could identify where one began and the other ended. Their shadows on the wall moved as one in their own rhythm. The sounds of their lovemaking filled the room, evidence of the passion and love they felt for one another. They soared to ecstasy and beyond, reaching heights to which neither had ever traveled. His muscles tensed Unable to hold back any longer, he gave himself to her, withholding nothing. Her scream of pleasure was confirmation that she'd received him with pure gratification.

Jackson laid next to Dale, and, with whatever strength he had left, pulled her to him. She cuddled into his large body and powerful arms. They both slowly drifted to sleep, satisfied their hearts' desires had been quelled. Before the sun would rise, the two made love again and again.

# Chapter 8

Craig leisurely walked into his office hoping for an uneventful day. But that wasn't to be the case.

"Sheriff," said his deputy, Matt. "We got an ID on that license plate."

Even though so much time had passed, the sheriff knew of what license plate his deputy spoke. It had been quite a mystery. The deputy came from the back with a piece of paper in his hand. Craig placed his hat on one of the hooks then went to read the paper.

"Is this right?" he asked.

"Yeah, he's pretty well-known," said Matt, smiling from ear-to-ear. He'd evidently heard of this man. The sheriff studied the information more closely.

"So, he's a big-time chef?" he asked.

"Not only is he a chef, Sir, but he owns a chain of restaurants around the country," Matt informed him. He liked to read the society column to keep up with what was going on outside their little town.

"Then shouldn't somebody be missing him about now?" The sheriff looked sternly at the deputy.

"Maybe he's supposed to be on vacation," said Matt.

Craig sat down at his desk. "It says here he has a wife. I'll call the local police department over there, let them know about the crash, and they can notify her."

He found the number in the directory and took the phone from the receiver. Matt couldn't wait to get to the barber shop to let them know they had a high-society man go missing right here in their little town.

It was morning, and Jackson lay in bed thinking of the bliss-filled night he'd experience with the most beautiful woman in the world. He turned to face her and wished she didn't have to go. He needed to feel her body next to his, and her lips on his lips. He just needed her period.

In another town, Darlene Marrell sat in her study. It had been three whole months since her husband went missing. She hadn't reported it in case this was another one of those stunts he'd pulled before. Some nonsense about leaving her. But before, he'd only gone for a few days, maybe even a few weeks, but not twelve. Maybe she should be concerned. She looked up as George made his way into the room. From the look on his face, he hadn't heard anything either.

"This is driving me insane," said Darlene after taking a drink of scotch. She'd been drinking all night. She was tall and slender, often mistaken for a model, and had platinum blonde hair and sinister blue eyes.

"Don't you think you should lighten up on the scotch?" said George.

Darlene glared at him. "What I think is that you need to find Jackson! He left out of here pissed that night." She took another swallow of liquor and George took a seat on the sofa.

"I have been meaning to ask you about that," he said. George was allowing the lawyer in him shine through.

"Listen, you overpaid ambulance chaser. If Jackson hadn't taken you on, that's exactly what you would be doing now. So get this straight. I want you to find my husband, not stand around here bothering me with questions. Now get out of my face!" she yelled.

George nodded and headed for the door, when the maid came through.

"Ma'am, there's a detective here to see you. Should I bring him back here?" she asked.

Darlene sat the glass down and hurried through the door. The maid and George tried to catch up to her.

"You have word about my husband?" she asked when she saw the detective.

"Mrs. Marrell?" he asked.

"Yes, I am! Do you have word on my husband?" she repeated.

"Yes, we do," he replied. "It seems he might have been in an accident."

She looked at him confused. "What the hell does that mean—might have been? Either he was or he wasn't!" she roared.

He shifted on his feet and gave her a stern look. George intervened. "Excuse me, Detective. My name is George Davis. I'm Mr. Marrells' attorney. If you could give us some details it would be very helpful."

"Mr. Davis, we got a call from a sheriff of a small town about two-hundred miles from here.

"Uh, maybe we should sit down," said George. This was more than a dispatch of information; this was also an inquiry, which may not be good.

The three of them went into the living room. The detective sat across from Darlene and George.

"I'm sorry to have to inform you that Mr. Marrell's automobile was in a very bad crash about three months ago," said the detective.

Darlene, who hadn't been looking at him, snapped her head up quickly and then fell into hysterics. "What!? God, no!" she cried.

George grabbed hold of her and looked at the detective. "Is he–?" George couldn't allow the words to come off his tongue.

"We don't know. The car was so badly damaged that the agency was only just able to track down your information based on a partial license plate. There have been no signs of Mr. Marrell anywhere. They searched the area and questioned the people there. No one has seen him. This is now a missing persons case."

81

Darlene buried her head into George's chest sobbing.

The detective took out a pad and pencil. "I need to ask you some questions," he said.

Darlene, who had recovered, began to fidget around, but George was calm and cool. "Of course," he said.

The detective directed his first question to Darlene. "Could you tell me about the events of the last time you saw him?"

She squirmed a bit. "He came home from seeing George here. We kind of got into an argument. It got heated, then he stomped out of the house. I ran to the door to catch him, but heard his car peel out of the driveway."

"What was the argument about?" asked the detective. He wrote down every word she said and took special note of her demeanor.

"Oh, I don't recall," Darlene replied. "It was over something little, as always. Lately it seemed that way with him." She rose from the couch and began to pace.

George tried to get her attention, but she was in a daze. He felt she was saying too much. The detective noticed this.

"Now, Mr. Davis," said the detective, "How was Mr. Marrell when he left you?"

"He was all right, just tired," said George. "He'd just returned from a business trip. He wanted to go home and relax." He turned to look at Darlene who was staring out of the window.

"Well, that didn't happen for whatever reason," said the detective. He stood to leave. "We'll be in touch. Please let us know if you think of anything else, or if you hear from Mr. Marrell."

"Thank you, Detective," said George.

The detective nodded his head and the maid showed him out.

"Wait!" Darlene cried. "George, get the name of the town. I'm going there, someone knows something and I'm going to find out if it's the last thing I do."

"Okay, but I'm going with you!" he insisted.

# Chapter 9

Dale was taking her evening walk, then she would go and join Jackson. She still wasn't sure it was a good idea for him to come back to the cabin until his memory returned. But he'd pleaded with her to let him come 'home' as he stated. She couldn't resist. And he wanted to walk with her that night, but she convinced him not to take the chance of someone seeing them.

The last bit of sunlight was dwindling out of sight as it was the end of dusk. Dale had walked all the way to the road and down it a little way. She heard the sound of a car getting nearer from behind and saw the beams from the headlights as it approached. As the car sped past, she stepped quickly to the side, narrowly escaping being struck by the speeding sedan. It was heading in the direction of town. "I know that has to be a city person," said Dale. "Folks don't drive like that around here."

She took a deep breath and steadied her heart. Duke and Banshee ran after the car barking their heads off. Then when the car moved farther away, they came back to see that Dale was okay. She calmed them down and continued her stroll.

"Damn it, Darlene!" George yelled. "Didn't you see that person back there?" He looked out the window to see if the person was all right.

He saw the woman step back into the road. He watched the dogs chasing them vanish from sight and Darlene continued to drive like a crazed lunatic.

"Shut up, George!" Darlene spat. "I want to get to this town and find out what happened to my husband. Anyway, the road is to drive on, not walk on."

"Look you two, this is bad for all of us. Jackson was my friend too," said Kevin, a longtime friend of Jackson's, who sat in the back seat.

"Don't you dare speak of him in the past-tense again!" Darlene screamed.

George ran his hand over his face. These two had gotten on his last nerve, and he couldn't wait to get to a hotel room separated from them. It had been a trying few hours.

"Whatever, Darlene," said Kevin.

"Don't get snippy with me, fella!" she said. "No one asked you to come. You just invited yourself," she reminded.

Kevin shifted in the back seat, then stared at her in through the rear view mirror. "Not this time Darlene, but we both know there have been times," said Kevin, obviously hinting at something.

George was looking through the window, but carefully listening to the two of them.

Darlene brought the car to a screeching halt, then turned completely around in her seat and stared daggers into Kevin. He pressed himself as far as he could into the upholstery.

"Kevin, I'll only tell you this once," she warned. "Shut the hell up."

Kevin nodded, knowing first-hand how violent she could get.

George never turned away from the window, something had caught his eye. There was a charred tree on the roadside. This must have been the place of impact, he thought. He would rent a car tomorrow and come back to investigate. Maybe he could find out who that person was walking back there. If the person walked like this routinely, he or she might know something. He felt the seat next to him creaking, as Darlene turned around and adjusted herself back into it. She put the car in drive and sped away, heading for the small town to get some information on her husband.

"Hey, you, we need some rooms—now!" Darlene said forcefully to the young woman behind the desk. She looked around, sneering at the hotel. She was expecting a five-star establishment, but seeing how quaint the town was, she knew better. But right now, luxury was lower on her list of importance than finding Jackson.

"How many rooms, Ma'am?" the young woman asked.

Darlene looked at her like she had just crawled from beneath a rock. "How many people do you see here?" She pointed to Kevin, then to George, and then herself.

The young woman looked at all three then to Darlene. She looked as if she would cry. "Three, Ma'am," she said.

"That's how many rooms we want," said Darlene.

"Yes, Ma'am," said the young woman. "I'm sorry Ma'am." She fumbled through the registry and found three rooms close together. She had them sign it and gave them their keys. George and Kevin shook their heads through the whole incident. Darlene could be very intimidating. They made their way up the stairs.

"All I want is to take a nice, hot, soothing bath," said Darlene. "Then I'm going to find that sheriff, and he'd better have some answers."

Kevin agreed with her, glad she was pointing that attitude toward someone else. George just wanted to get out of ear shot of her mouth. He had plans of his own.

Darlene stomped into the sheriff's office and stopped in front of the largest desk. "Are you the sheriff of this place?" she asked.

Craig looked up from his newspaper at the tall, slim blonde. He immediately rose to his feet. "Yes, Ma'am. What can I do for ya?" he asked.

She put her hand on her hip. "What you can do is tell me where in the hell is my husband?" she snapped.

Craig tilted his head to one side and figured everything out. "You must be Mrs. Marrell, the wife of our missing stranger," he said.

"That's right," she said. "But there are two things I want you to get straight. He isn't a stranger and he'd better not be missing much longer." She stared daggers at the small town sheriff.

He took in a deep breath and let it out slowly, scratching his head. Why did this man come to his town to go missing? Better yet, why did he have to have this woman for a wife? He knew already she was trouble.

Meanwhile, George asked the desk clerk at the hotel where was the nearest car rental agency. She told him the name of the place and gave him directions. He tipped her two twenty dollar bills. One for her patience with Darlene, and the other because he felt like it.

He went back to his room. He was glad to be rid of Darlene's ranting. He took a hot shower to calm his nerves, then waited until he heard Darlene leave her own room. She did so with Kevin right at her side. He didn't want either one to know of his plans for the next day. He knew what time she got up, which would be late. By that time, he would have left town to do some investigation without any distractions.

When George arrived at the rental car agency, a man came out of an office to greet him. "Hiya. You one of them strangers looking for the guy in that accident?"

George kept a blank face. "I'm looking to rent a car, and if possible, maybe you can give me some information," he said. "I can make it worth your while." George knew his type. He dug into his pocket and brought out his wallet.

The man looked around to make sure they were alone. "What do ya' you need?" he asked, straight out.

George smiled and began to run his thumb over the bills. The man wiped his mouth. He had never seen that much money in his life.

"I saw someone walking along the road near the accident site," said George. "You wouldn't know who that person might be—would you?" He slid out a couple of bills and laid them on the counter.

"Yeah, I know her," said the man.

"Her?" George asked.

The man nodded. "Her name's Dale. Dale Banner," he told him. "She's lives out there by herself. Has for years. Only comes to town to get groceries and such. In fact, she's due in tomorrow."

George thought for a moment. "How do you know it was her?" he asked. "Could have been anyone."

"Everybody knows she takes a walk same time every night," said the man.

"So she could have seen or heard something?" George asked.

"Naw!" the man replied. "Not that night. Word about town is that she was sick in bed. That's what she told the sheriff."

"Well, then she wouldn't have seen anything," said George while pushing the money more toward the man. The man took it and smiled happily.

George looked at some of the cars for rent.

"She said her dogs barked at some noise then calmed down," said the man. "Then she said she heard the explosion from her front porch when she came out to see what her dogs were barking for."

George looked back at him with that added information. "So she just heard something from a distance," he mumbled mostly to himself.

"You know, the deputy wasn't convinced of that," said the man. "And even the sheriff felt she was holding something back. But she convinced them both that she knew nothin' more than she told'em."

"I think I would like that car if I may, and a map of this area," said George. He told the man he would pick it up in the morning, early. He also explained that this conversation never happened and gave him some more money to keep his mouth shut.

Later, George met Darlene and Kevin at a diner. They sat at a corner booth and George stared through the window, deep in thought. He'd made some progress. The guy at the car rental place may have been more helpful than he knew. This Dale woman walked faithfully every night, but by some chance, she skipped that particular night. Even the sheriff found her story suspicious. She's due in town tomorrow. Maybe he could secretly follow her home and ask her some questions in private. Too many people around might spook her, then he'd get nowhere.

"Oh, this place is just the most backwards place I've ever been!"

George, who had retreated into his thoughts due to Darlene's constant yammering, was just pulled back out of them for the same reason.

"Darlene, don't make them any angrier than you have already," Kevin cautioned, giving the waitress a huge smile. "I don't want them doing anything to my food," he said once the waitress had gone.

"They wouldn't dare," Darlene growled.

"Yeah, they would," Kevin said under his breath and took a sip of water.

Darlene took a big drink of water. She'd heard about people coming up missing in small towns like this. She then gave the waitress a phony smile. The woman just turned and walked away. The damage had been done.

"Anyway, I spoke to the sheriff," said Darlene to George.

"So what did he have to say?" he humored her.

"Nothing we don't already know. I tell you of all the places in the world, why did Jackson have to pick this God-forsaken place to disappear?" She dug in her purse and pulled out her compact. All this excitement was too much for her looks. George looked at her with some annoyance.

"This 'God-forsaken place', as you called it, had nothing to do with Jackson's disappearance and you know it."

Kevin looked over at George then down to his plate. He knew when George spoke in that tone, he'd had enough.

"I have no idea what you are talking about," said Darlene. She leaned back and stared blankly at him. Kevin shifted in his seat.

"Fine, have it your way," said George. "Because I sure as hell will." He then looked up at the waitress, who had arrived with their food. She smiled as she set his plate and Kevin's before them. They thanked her.

Darlene eyes narrowed. George had something up his sleeves, she just knew it. She'd have to keep a close eye on him. She turned to see to the waitress setting her plate before her, and the look the waitress gave convinced her she wasn't so hungry anymore. George chuckled inwardly. He was going to have to pull off a slick move tomorrow, Darlene was no fool. He took an enjoyable bite of his food.

Darlene looked at Kevin, who was enjoying his meal also. She looked down at hers and then to the waitress who was now behind the counter. She raised a glass with a smile on her face. Darlene knew then, it was a good idea to leave it. She took a sip of water, thinking maybe she could get something somewhere else. And this time she'd be nicer if it killed her.

When the trio got back to the hotel, Darlene chattered on, but also observed George with great interest. He was too quiet.

George knew he had to make some plans with Darlene or she would get suspicious. So he stopped outside her door for a chat.

"Can Kevin and I come in for a minute?" he asked. "We aren't getting anywhere with this sheriff. He doesn't know anything. Maybe some of the townspeople can help us better."

Darlene was thrown off guard. That's what he wanted.

"Sure! I was beginning to wonder about you," she said. She opened the door and let them inside. George was playing his role, but Kevin just wanted to go to bed.

"I was thinking," said George. "Do you have a picture of Jackson?"

Kevin threw himself on the bed, grinning sheepishly, which got him a glare from Darlene.

"Yes. Why?" she asked, digging through her purse. She found one, and took a moment to stare at it. Then she handed it to George. He waved her off.

"I need you to get flyers made of this picture," he said. "We can circulate them through town. Maybe someone has seen or heard something, they just didn't know it."

Darlene stared at him for a moment then nodded her head. "Okay," she said. "That sounds like a great idea. What will you be up to in the meantime?"

"I'm going to try to light a fire under the sheriff," he replied. "Then I'm going out to the accident site to see what I can find. Although, I trust these guys did a thorough job." This would keep her busy, he thought—and off his back for a while, giving him time to talk with Miss Banner.

"All right," she said. "Well, I'm going to turn in. We've got a long day ahead of us."

Darlene glared at Kevin, who'd fallen asleep while she and George were taking care of business. George gave him a kick on his foot, waking him with a start.

When the two men had gone, Darlene went to the window and looked out over the town. Then she looked down at his picture. "Where are you Jackson?" she whispered.

## Chapter 10

Morning had come and Dale left Jackson peacefully sleeping. She didn't want to leave his side, but she had to get to town for her usual shopping. If she didn't, it could cast suspicion. She didn't mind that people like Craig were concerned about her, but she had to think about Jackson. She drove into town, unaware of the excitement coursing through it.

Dale parked in front of the grocery store as she always did and got out to go inside. But this time, Deputy Matt came over to her form the station across the street. Immediately, she tried to think of a way to shove him off without hurting his feelings.

"Hi, Dale," he said.

"Hello, Matt," she said, continuing to the door.

"Did you hear?" He was anxious to tell her of the commotion going around town.

"Now Matt, how many times do I have to tell you, I don't listen to gossip," she gently scolded.

"Oh, well," he said aloud to himself as he turned away. "I just wanted to tell her about the wife of the missing man."

Dale paused and looked over her shoulder. But Matt was heading back to the station.

Just then, the man from the rental car agency walked up to George who was on the sidewalk nearby. "Hey, Mister," he said. "There she goes, inside the grocery store."

George just got a glimpse of her back as she entered, but it didn't matter. He was more interested in which car was hers.

"Is that her car parked right in front?" he asked.

"Yes sir, it certainly is," he confirmed.

"I'll be picking up that rental now," said George.

Dale began to fill her cart with what was on her list. She would sometimes have it delivered, but wouldn't take the risk since Jackson had returned to the cabin.

"I guess you haven't heard about the commotion going on in town," said Hank. He was reading his newspaper and only half-way watching Dale. He was never convinced she didn't know of the missing man's whereabouts. He felt because Craig carried a torch for her, he needed to believe she wouldn't lie to him in such a manner.

"No," said Dale. "And I really don't want to get into anyone else's business," she told him.

"Oh, this ain't just anyone's business," he said. "The whole town is in an uproar."

It may have been the way he phrased it, or the tone of his voice that made Dale stop what she was doing and look at him. "What do you mean?" she asked. His eyebrows lifted and he set his newspaper down on the counter. He was pleased he had gotten her attention.

"Well, you remember that car crash three months ago, near your place?" he said, watching her intensely.

Her face was solemn. "Yes, I remember," she said. "How could anyone forget?"

"Right," he said with a hint of sarcasm. "Anyway, yesterday there was finally a hit on that license plate. Matt showed the sheriff," he told her.

She felt her heart sink to the pit of her stomach. If it wasn't for her beautiful brown skin, she would have turned pale.

"So who was it that went missing?" she asked, a lump in her throat.

"Some high-society guy," he said. "Matt knows more about him than anyone. Said he had read up on him," he told her.

"But," she said, shaking her head. "Why didn't anyone report him missing?" She knew that just like Matt's, Hank's mouth couldn't hold water if it had to. And she had to know if he knew any more.

"His wife said he had done this before when they had arguments," he informed her. But Dale didn't hear anything past the word 'wife'.

"Wife?" she repeated. She said it very softly, but it didn't stop Hank from hearing it or from noticing her reaction.

"Yes, there are three of them in town," he told her. "The wife and two friends of his."

Her head lifted quickly. "In town now?" she asked.

"Yes, right now," said Hank. "In fact, they're passing out flyers with his picture on it."

Dale felt as if her legs would buckle under her. She rushed form the building and jumped in the car. Hank ran behind her and watched her peel out of town once again. Now he knew for sure that she knew something. He hurried over to the sheriff's office.

"Craig!" he said as burst through the doors. "I tell you Dale is hiding that man up there at her cabin."

The sheriff had been leaning back in his chair, feet propped up on the desk. He quickly took them down and leaned in to hear what Hank had to say.

"What are you going on about, Hank?" he asked. "How many times have we gone over this?"

But Hank wasn't going to give in this time. "I'm telling you, Craig, something is going on out there." He was very annoyed with Craig's reaction.

"Okay," said Craig. "Tell me what's going on."

Hank sat down in the chair in front of Craig's desk. "I told Dale that the man's wife is in town," he said. "She nearly passed out when I told her. Then, just like that one day, she ran out the door and sped off in a hurry. Left without her stuff."

The sheriff then came to his feet. He went to the window and saw the wife and one of the other men in her party walking toward the rental car agency. He took notice that the lawyer wasn't with them.

Matt also noticed.

"I'm telling you," said Darlene, "that George is on to something. That's why he sent us on this little distraction. It was to get us out of the way."

She and Kevin watched George pull away in a rental car. He apparently hadn't noticed them. They had left the hotel early to get the flyers made and George thought they were still sleeping. That was a mistake.

"Well, maybe he's keeping a tight lip until he gets more information," said Kevin. "That way he doesn't get your hopes up high."

"I don't give a damn, what his reasons are!" Darlene yelled. "He's onto something and he's keeping me out of the loop. Jackson is my husband. I need to know everything that there is to know. And I promise you this, I will." She then stormed into the agency to get her own information. Kevin looked up at the sky thinking, why him?

'Wife' continued to echo in Dale's mind. He really is married. Tears filled her eyes as she drove, and she had to keep wiping them away to see the road. Jackson… her mind called out. She needed to get back to him quickly. She needed to feel his body next to hers. She needed to feel his lips on hers. She just needed him period. She pulled onto the winding road that led to the cabin. When she came around the bend, she saw Jackson and the dogs. She ran from the car and into his waiting arms. He held her tight.

"Why didn't you wake me before you left?" he asked. He hooked her chin with his finger and tilted her head up to face him.

She smiled. "I'm sorry, I didn't want to wake you," she said.

But Jackson's own smile faded. "You've been crying, Dale. What's wrong? What's happened?"

At that time, Duke and Banshee were lying down relaxing. But suddenly they came to their feet and began to bark. Dale could hear what was coming before she could see it. She turned her head to watch. Both Jackson and Dale watched as a car approached.

George couldn't believe his eyes, but he recognized his old friend, Jackson. He pulled the car up to the couple. There was something else he noticed. Jackson had a serene expression on his face as he held the woman he had followed from town. He had never seen that look on his friend before.

He cut the car off and was almost hesitant to leave it. One reason was the two huge dogs at his door. The second reason was that Jackson was alive and hadn't tried to contact them. There must have been a reason.

Dale made the dogs lie down quietly and George got out of the car.

"Jackson? Is that you?" asked George.

Dale felt her heart rip in two. All she had feared was coming to pass.

"You know me?" Jackson asked.

George was puzzled. Jackson truly didn't recognize him. "Yes, of course I know you," he said with care, realizing his friend was not himself. "I'm your friend, and I'm also your lawyer. We've gone crazy looking for you," George explained. "What happened?"

It was more than Dale could bear. She turned away. She knew it was a fantasy they were living and that sooner or later they would be found out.

"As far as I know, I was in a car accident and woke up here," said Jackson.

"Why didn't you contact us to let us know you were all right?" asked George.

"I didn't know who I was," said Jackson. "I found a piece of paper with the name Jackson on it, and assumed it was me." I still don't know a thing. He told him.

George looked harshly at Dale. "That explains why he didn't let anyone know that he was alive. What was your reason?" George asked with a harsh tone. He started toward Dale but Jackson grabbed George's arm.

"Don't ever speak to her that way again," Jackson warned. He didn't care who this man claimed to be, he didn't know him, so he didn't owe him. Dale was the one who held his heart, and no one was going to walk into their lives and disrespect her.

"All right, Jackson," George said, recognizing his friend's old temperament. "I just want to know what happened. Why hasn't she notified the police? Have you even seen a doctor?"

"For your information, I didn't want to see a doctor, and she urged me to let her tell the sheriff I was here. But I made her promise not to. If you want to jump down someone's throat, jump down mine," said Jackson sternly.

George felt a familiar fear rise within him. Jackson could always do that. His temper was infamous in their group of friends.

"Okay, calm down Jackson," he said. "Please except my apology," he said to Dale.

"It's all right," she said with a hint of sadness.

107

George then understood there was something special between these two. The dogs began to whine, but Dale quieted them.

"Okay, Jackson. I don't understand," said George. "Why wouldn't you want anyone to know where you were? Or that you were alive?" George asked.

"I would like that answer myself," said the sheriff, just approaching from the back of the cabin.

Dale felt her legs weaken. Craig came to face her and stopped. She saw in his eyes the betrayal he felt. She couldn't bear any of it any longer and collapsed. Craig grabbed her before she touched the ground, but Jackson raced over and took her away from him. He swept her into his arms and carried her into the cabin.

George stepped to Craig's side.

"You found your man," said Craig. "When will ya'll be leaving these parts?" He never looked George's way.

"I suppose that's up to Jackson," said George. "And as far as I can see, that may not be an easy decision."

Whether Jackson could recall his past or not, George could tell he was in love with this woman.

"I beg to differ," said a shrill voice behind them. Darlene and Kevin arrived just in time to witness Jackson taking Dale into the house. The man at the car rental place had been easily persuaded. And it only cost them fifty bucks.

# Chapter 11

"Dale… Dale…" a voice called out. She fought her way through the dense shroud of darkness that engulfed her. The voice grew nearer. She felt something wet and cool on her forehead. Her eyes slowly opened, then strained to see between the slits that shielded them from the sun light.

"Jackson," she breathed.

"Yes, Sweet Lady, it's me," he replied.

Her eyes began to widen. "Where is your friend?" she asked, knowing their time together had run its course.

"Right here with me," he said.

She looked at him with such love, it nearly broke his heart. He knew what she meant, but he didn't know that man outside. She was all he knew.

"That is so sweet of you, Jackson," but you and I both know that this is our ending." She touched the side of his face with one of her hands and gazed deep into his eyes. "You must go home and get your life back together," she said.

He took her hand into his own, then lifted it to his lips and kissed it gently.

Tears filled her eyes. He turned away from her, not able to bear the pain in his heart. He walked through the door and left. She turned onto her side, away from the door, not wanting to see him walk out of her life, and she wept.

"Darlene, what the hell are you doing here?" asked George.

"What am I doing here?" she asked with utter confusion. "Did he just asked me what am I doing here?"

"Yes, he did," said Kevin.

"I had this under control," said George. "You should leave. And don't make a scene."

Darlene raised a brow and stared him down. But then her eyes grew large as she looked past him.

"Jackson… Jackson. Is that you baby?" Her pace increasing as she headed to him.

He didn't know her at all. He looked at her without any emotions. She ran up the steps and threw her arms around his neck, squeezing him tight. He was motionless. He looked at George, confused. He was the only other person he knew in this whole charade.

"Darlene, let him go," George said. She pulled away from Jackson, staring at his blank eyes. Her eyebrows furrowed, as she could see there was something different about him.

"What is going on George?" She turned her head in his direction, removing her arms from around Jackson's neck.

"This is why I wish you had let me handle this," he said. "He doesn't know you. His memory is gone."

Her mouth slid open and looked from George to Jackson, who just stared at her indifferently. Then something caught her eyes. The woman who he had carried into the house was standing just beyond the door. Her anger nearly erupted.

"His memory is lost, huh?" she spat. "But I bet he hasn't forgot how to screw, isn't that right Jackson?"

"Look lady," said Jackson, "and I'm being kind calling you that, what I do in my personal life doesn't concern you."

Darlene's mouth fell open. George quickly grabbed her and walked her off the porch before she said something else regretful. Jackson just about had enough of this farce.

Craig slowly walked by the two and stepped up on the porch, facing off with Jackson. "If you care as much as I think you do, you'll go with your people and get yourself straightened out."

"I've already figured that out, sheriff," said Jackson. "Please do me a favor..." his voice nearly broke.

"I know," said Craig, "and I will. Always have. Just get yourself whole."

Jackson never turned to see Dale standing at the door wiping the tears rolling down her cheeks. He left the porch and walked toward the two screaming at each other. "You two can stop the bickering, I'm going with you," he said. Then he got into George's car.

Darlene was confused at first, but she looked up at the cabin and made a vow to come back to deal with the whore who obviously slept with her husband. She beckoned for Kevin to come along and both cars left.

Dale slowly came out of the cabin, and watched Jackson leave her life forever. Craig watched her with great sympathy. He knew how much she missed Thaddeus. It gets lonely out here. But that's the way she wanted it… at least it's the way she used to want it.

"I'm sorry Dale… so sorry," said Craig stepping onto the porch. Dale fell into his arms and cried.

When Jackson, George, Darlene, and Kevin returned to town, word had already been spread that the famous chef had been at Dale's cabin all the time. A crowd had formed around their hotel and Matt tried to disperse them. But people still gathered on the street, even when the hotel owner brought out his shotgun and warned everyone to leave his guests alone.

Jackson felt terrible knowing he'd brought this down on Dale. He wanted to slip away and convince her to run off with him. But his urging her to keep quiet in the first place had got her in this mess. He didn't want to cause her any more trouble.

Jackson took the room next to George's, which infuriated Darlene. She felt that, as her husband, he should have shared her room, and her bed. But he fiercely protested.

The next morning, the group left early, before the sun rose. It was a long trip home. And when they pulled into the driveway of Jackson's home, something was very familiar to him.

He knew at once that he'd been there before. Maybe his memory was resurfacing. The car came to a stop and the others got out. Jackson was the last to exit. He went to take a step, but became very dizzy, as if the world was turning upside down. Then he had a flashback...

He was running from the house. He slammed the door behind him. He remembered the house shaking from the force. He was fumbling to unlock the vehicle. He was furious with anger. Finally, he got in and sped away....

"Jackson?" George touched him on the shoulder, snapping him out of his trance.

"I think I remember something," said Jackson.

"What was it?" asked George, anxiously.

Darlene and Kevin were nearly at door of the house when they realized Jackson and George were still standing by the car.

"Come on you two," she barked.

The two men looked on as she went into the house and then returned to their conversation.

"I remember rushing out of the house and speeding out of here. I was very angry," said Jackson.

George listened very intensely. "Do you remember what it was you were angry about?" he asked. He was very concerned.

"No," said Jackson. "Maybe coming here was a good idea. It might trigger my complete memory, then I can get back to Dale."

George shook his head. "Look Jackson, I think mentioning her name is a bad idea, if you want to live in serenity around here."

Jackson was not amused. "I want something to be straight with you and with everyone else around here." He came face to face with George. "I'm only here to get back my memory. Then I leave, so I can be with the woman I love. She is the one in my heart, not that siren in there. Got it?"

George took a step backward. "That may not be so easy, Jackson. Legally, you're still married. And

knowing Darlene, she'll make your life a living hell."
George began counseling him. Jackson straightened
up and glared at him.

"I can deal with that as long as I'm with Dale,"
he insisted, taking a defiant stance.

George shook his head again. "Let me make this
plainer," he said. "Darlene won't just make your life a
living hell, but she'll do it to Dale as well. Is that what
you want?" George saw by the expression on
Jackson's face that he now understood.

"Fine," he snapped before walking away.

George exhaled. This was going to be the most
stressful ordeal yet.

Jackson went into the house he would have to
call home. As he walked through the door, he paused.
There was something about this area as well. His eyes
scanned it over and came to rest on the floor. He
stared at that spot as images began to fill his mind.
This was the place in his recurring dreams…

He'd just walked in… It had been a long day…
He wanted a hot bath and a stiff drink… The mail
was on the floor….

"Jackson, you all right?" asked George.

Jackson came out of the daydream with a start.
"Yeah, I'm fine," he said. He then headed for the den.

George watched him navigate the house without assistance. He wondered how much he really knew. Was his amnesia an act, or was he beginning to recall his memories?

Kevin was sitting at the bar drinking a bottle of beer. His eyes shot up when he saw Jackson walk in. Kevin hadn't spoken to Jackson since they found him. He felt awkward around him. Jackson stared back at him with interest.

"Who are you?" Jackson inquired while taking a beer for himself.

Kevin watched him pour some whiskey into a shot glass, just like he always had.

George observed from the doorway.

"I'm Kevin, your best friend."

Jackson stared at the man with a curious look on his face, which made Kevin him more nervous. Jackson threw down the shot and chased it with a swig of beer before turning to George. "I thought you told me you were my best friend?"

"No, I told you I was your friend and lawyer," George corrected. He left his observation post and joined the men at the bar.

Jackson took a long hard look at the two of them. In the back of his mind, he felt that one of them one wasn't as much of a friend as he claimed to be. Was it a gut feeling, or a memory?

## Chapter 12

Three months had passed since Jackson returned to his other life. Dale drove away from the town she had now come to dread and headed home. The whole town knew she'd been keeping the missing man a secret. And they knew she had lied to the sheriff, her good friend. Every time she went into town, it seemed the business would pick up at the little grocery store. She could feel the patrons' eyes digging into her like knives as they stopped and stared and whispered behind her back.

But today was different. Almost no one knew she was there. She hadn't been feeling well since Jackson left. It left a void in her life. Spending time with

Jackson, had begun to sooth the pain she felt from the loss of Thad. Now she had lost them both.

She pulled up at home and was greeted by Duke and Banshee. She paused before going inside and took a lingering look around the place she'd called home for so long. It had been a place of refuge.

Thad had built it for her from a simple dream she relayed to him. Tears stung her eyes. She was going to miss this place dearly. But she could no longer bare to live there. It was supposed to be filled with love, but instead was a source of pain.

She wiped the tears from her eyes and thought about Jackson. She wondered how he was doing, if he ever thought about her, and whether he had regained his memory. She was certain that he had, because he hadn't tried to contact her. Why would he when he had such a gorgeous wife? Then she looked down at her stomach and ran her hand gently over it.

The doctor had confirmed her feelings. She was three months pregnant with Jackson's child. She sat in her chair on the porch, rubbing her stomach and rocking, a smile etched on her face. How easy it was to conceive his child. Their child. She may not have him in her life anymore, but she had a part of him.

She rose from the chair and went inside to make plans to leave this phase of her life behind.

Jackson was at his business office and sat behind his desk. He smiled, knowing Dale would laugh at the irony of it all. She'd wondered how he knew how to set a fancy dinner table, and cook special meals. It was his profession. In fact, he owned several restaurants in other cities, but this one was his first. It took him only a week to get back into the swing of things. It was like he had never left.

He remembered a lot about work and his profession, but some other things were still lost to him. Around the house, flashbacks and familiarity would guide him. Those thoughts of the night of the accident, however, were still incomplete. He would get as far as the bedroom door and everything would go blank but for his speeding angrily away.

But he was most puzzled by the fact that he remembered nearly everything except his love for Darlene. No matter how much he tried reintroduce himself as her husband, he just wasn't feeling it. He knew it was hurting her and wondered what kind of a person he had been before. How could he have married such a self-centered, obnoxious, inconsiderate, conniving and clueless woman?

She had zero understanding. No matter how much you tried to explain things, she just didn't get it. So what did that say about what kind of person he had been? Not much, as far as he was concerned.

His love for Dale only accented his rejection. Yes, Darlene was a very attractive woman, but she was no lady. There was only surface, no depth to her at all. She was like a beautiful rose you'd pick only to be stuck by its unseen thorns.

He dreaded going home or even being there when she arrived. He knew what the outcome would always be; an argument. Each night he came home, he would get the mail from the floor and toss it on his desk, just like the dream. But instead of going upstairs, where he rarely went, he would head for the bar for a drink and fall asleep in the chair.

As for Kevin and George, he had gut feelings about them too. They were always dropping by to see if he remembered anything new. Sometimes he wondered if they were concerned for him or afraid of something.

His heart was heavy from missing Dale. He'd picked up the phone a thousand times, but George's warning stuck with him. He didn't want to bring her anymore pain than he already had. So he planned a way to get in touch with secretly.

It had been over three months and he decided to go see her. He'd been in a fight with Darlene, as was the routine. He was ready to toss this charade. He drove the hours it took to get back to Dale, only to discover she was no longer there. Everything was different.

The caretaker told him everything except her whereabouts. He either didn't know or wasn't saying. Unbeknownst to Jackson, he'd only missed Dale by a few days. He wanted to ask the sheriff, but he didn't think it wasn't a good idea. So he turned back home.

But Darlene had him followed. She knew that sooner or later he would make the mistake of trying see Dale. She was told of his visit, but she didn't know that Dale had moved. She decided to take matters into her own hands. She went to pay Dale a visit. She planned to tell her, in no uncertain terms, to stay away from her husband.

She drove to Dale's cabin but there was no sign of Dale. Instead, a man appeared. Dale has a man! she thought excitedly. This little visit may prove rewarding after all.

She stepped out of her car, feeling a little triumphant, and began to walk toward the cabin. But when the man stepped into view, she was surprised to find it was the sheriff in plain clothes. Darlene smiled sheepishly.

"Howdy Ma'am," said Craig. "What are you doin' so far away from home?"

"I came to pay Dale Banner a visit," she confessed. "I want to warn her to stay away from my husband."

"Seems to me, you should be havin' this talk with your husband," said Craig. "Dale hasn't seen him in months."

"My husband, as you called him, doesn't act like a husband," said Darlene. "And I think it's because of Dale. I think they've been seeing each other in secret. I had him followed, and he was here yesterday."

Craig was confused. "You say he was here yesterday, and saw Dale?" he asked, taking off his hat and scratching his head.

Darlene just nodded.

"That can't be," said Craig with a chuckle.

Her eyes narrowed. She didn't find anything humorous about this. She felt a curse coming on.

"You see, Dale moved out a little over a week ago," said Craig. "She sold this place and ain't been heard of since. If your husband came here, he didn't see Dale."

Now Darlene was confused. "Are you sure she sold this place?"

"I sure am," he said. "Because she sold it to me."

Darlene was somewhat relieved, but not totally. "Well, that doesn't change much," she said.

She came to stand below him as he sat down on the step. He looked her over. She certainly was a beauty, that he couldn't deny. Craig followed her eyes as she looked out at the lake. In a way, he felt sorry for this one. She didn't quite understand. All that beauty, but no heart to go along with it.

"What do you mean it doesn't change much?" he asked.

Being this close and alone with the sheriff had turned the tides in Darlene's eyes. He now had the upper hand. She stared into his eyes. They were wise. She felt a little intimidated. No one had ever made her feel that way before.

"Dale might be gone," said Darlene, "but it doesn't keep Jackson from wanting her. If anything, he probably wants her more. She's like this ghost that stands between us." She tried to sound hurt.

Craig's eyes narrowed as he listened. "That woman has a name," he reminded her. "And as far as her bein' between you and your husband. I don't think so. I think there's more to it than that." He stood up and moved up the stairs.

Darlene paused for a moment. She'd had a realization when she heard his tone. "Well, I'll be damned. You're in love with this woman too!"

"That's my business and none of yours," he said.

Darlene eased up the steps and inched closer to him. She noticed how his t-shirt and tight jeans showed off his well-kept body. For an older guy, he was very well put together. "Well, it may not be my business," she said, "but you and I are in the same boat." She began to run her finger up and down his chest.

He flinched. It was doing something to him. "What boat is that?" he asked.

She moved up to the step below him and pressed her body against his. "The out-of-love boat. We love them but they love each other." She hooked her finger in the collar of his shirt and pulled it downward to expose his chest.

Craig stepped back and looked at her, hard. She was so right. Dale never returned his affection. He led her up to the top step with him. Her face was now near his. Her sweet aroma consumed him. He felt his body responding to this vixen. She was the devil in disguise, enticing him. He should walk away and send her home to her husband. But it had been a long time for him.

His mouth soon covered hers. He parted her lips with his tongue. She surrendered into his arms, wanting everything this man could give her... everything her husband refused to give.

Craig picked her up and carried her into the cabin. They had the roughest sex of their lives, releasing all of their pent-up frustrations. Neither loved the other, so it really didn't matter what they did to get the job done.

Darlene didn't leave until morning. And she drove away without a backwards look, never to come this way again.

Craig laid silently in bed, thinking about what he had done. In a moment of weakness, he'd gone against everything he believed in. He'd slept with another man's wife.

He'd discovered something about her that was nagging at him. It was true what they say about strange bed fellows. It was so easy for her to sleep with him... especially after she caught on to his love for Dale. It was as if their little tryst wasn't so much to ease her pain as it was for revenge. By sleeping with him, she now had something with which to taunt Jackson and Dale.

He eased up in bed, thinking. His gut told him something. Jackson didn't have amnesia. He was blocking something out—something that had him running into the night and caused his crash. Could it have been because of Darlene?

## Chapter 13

Jackson looked over the information from the detective he'd hired to find Dale. He'd told the detective the townspeople would probably tell him what he needed. But they hadn't been as helpful as he'd hoped. They hadn't seemed to know anything. Jackson paid him, and thanked him for trying. He slumped behind his desk, dejected.

"Did he take it badly?" Darlene asked, holding the package the detective gave her.

"Just the way you guessed. I convinced him I wasn't able to find anything. But as you will see, I most certainly did."

Darlene took a bulky envelope from her desk and tossed it to the detective.

He opened it and made sure it contained the amount they'd agreed on. He'd known Darlene for a while, so when Jackson called him, he took the opportunity to make this separate arrangement.

"If I were you," said Darlene, "I would leave here and never come back. Because if Jackson ever finds out that you double-crossed him, it won't be pretty. And needless to say, don't even think about crossing me."

He registered what she was saying and agreed she was right. He'd seen Jackson. And he had no desire to stick around for him to find out. "Yeah, I get the picture," he said nervously.

Dale sat in her rocker, caressing her stomach and speaking to the child developing inside. She couldn't wait to see what she was going to have. She decided not to know the gender until the birth. It was to be a little surprise for herself. Only one other person outside the doctor's office knew the gender. He'd been there for support when she had the ultrasound. It was her friend Craig.

She researched names for both boys and girls. She was relaxed and happy in her new place—in a city far from where she once lived.

It was a simple little place enough for the two of them. There were no plans for a man in her life unless she had a son. She'd experienced the bliss of having two wonderful men in her life, and the agony of losing them both. Her first love had given her precious memories. Her second love had gone on to a life he had once forgotten. In its own way, this one was the hardest, because she was haunted every night by thoughts of him holding his wife in his arms, kissing his wife as he had once kissed her, and even of them making love. It was torture.

The doorbell rang, breaking Dale from her thoughts. She left the comfort of her chair and went to answer the door. She looked through the peep hole before opening the door. The person on the other side looked familiar, but it couldn't be.

"Yes, may I help you?" asked Dale.

"Are you Dale Banner?" asked Darlene.

Dale opened the door wider. Yes, she looked very familiar. "Who are you—may I ask?" Dale was being very cautious.

"Yes, you may. I'm Darlene Marrell. My husband is Jackson, you saved his life."

Dale's heart sunk. She felt as if she would faint. If she found her, then Jackson surly could.

"How did you find me?" Dale snapped, gathering herself.

Darlene's eyes began to darken. How dare she talk to her like this? Then she calmed herself, she needed to get inside so as not to make a scene. Dale had moved into a quaint community, a lot different from being secluded in the back woods.

"I had to find you," said Darlene. "There is something I have to tell you about Jackson. But I don't want to do it out here, if you don't mind." She was a very good actress.

"Oh, yes, come in please," said Dale.

Darlene could sense the worry in her voice. She moved into the house swiftly. She sauntered in and stared Dale down as she closed the door. She immediately noticed something. Dale was a little thick around the middle.

Dale turned to face her, waiting for the worst. She got it, but not exactly what she had expected.

"Cute house," Darlene sneered.

Dale sat down, sensing something wasn't right. "Thank you," she said politely. But her patience was thinning. She got the feeling this wasn't a courtesy call. "What about Jackson? Is he all right? Has his memory come back? Excuse my manners... please sit."

Dale rambled on nervously. Darlene just glared then took a seat. She looked around the small house.

"To answer your questions," said Darlene, "Jackson is fine. And no, he hasn't regained his full memory. This is why I'm here. I want you to stay away from him. I hope you enjoyed that little time you spent with him, because there will be no more."

Dale was shocked. She sat back in her chair and thought long and hard before responding. "Okay, first of all, how dare you come into my house under false pretenses? You made me think something was wrong with Jackson."

Darlene's eyes grew wide. She didn't think the country bumpkin had it in her. "You listen here–" she tried to interrupt.

"No, you listen," Dale said firmly. "You came into my house, and now you're going to hear me out. I haven't seen or heard from Jackson in nearly four months, and by now, I don't expect to. So go back and enjoy your husband, and stop hounding me."

Darlene stood up towering over the other woman. "I'll say this once again," said Darlene, "stay away from my husband." She had to get the last word in, no matter how feeble.

Dale rolled her eyes and opened the door for Darlene to leave. Darlene stood there for a moment, then headed for the door. But she suddenly paused when she realized something. The sunlight from outside shined through the lightweight dress that Dale was wearing. It outlined her protruding stomach. She wasn't simply thick in the middle; it was a baby bump.

"A baby–" said Darlene. "You're having a baby?"

Dale pointed to the door. "Get out of my house. You have Jackson, now go! Right now!" she screamed.

Darlene knew this wasn't a good time to press the matter. She'd find out later if that baby belonged to Jackson. She rushed out the door and Dale slammed it behind her. Darlene got in the car and drove away. She would have to get ahold of that private investigator. There were some things he'd omitted from the results of his investigation. She never saw the car pull into the spot she had just left. Nor did she see the man who got out and watched her drive away before Dale welcomed him into her house.

Jackson sat in the lounge at home. He had just finished his nightly drink when he felt the house vibrate. He groaned. He knew what that meant. She was home and she was angry. He got up to make it to his room before she found him.

"Jackson!" her voice rang through the house.

He fell back into his seat and struggled to get up again. Just then, Darlene flew into the room and began beating on him. He tried to block her hits.

"You bastard!" she screamed.

He finally caught her hands and got a good grip. He glared into her angry eyes. "Do not ever raise your hands to me again," he warned. His voice was low and deep. She could see he was very serious.

"Let me go!" she yelled.

He released her arms and rose from the chair. He looked her up and down, then shook his head and headed for the stairs.

"I hate you!" Darlene continued. "And I hate that little whore of yours!"

Those last words made him stop and turn around. She was crying. "Whore? Who are you talking about? I haven't been with anyone," he said.

"Dale Banner!" she snapped, rubbing her wrists.

"Dale? Why are you bringing up Dale?" he asked. "I haven't seen her in months."

Now she was sniffling. "No. But a month ago you tried," she said.

His face went through a chain of expressions, then finally came to one that told her he was angry.

"How would you know that, Darlene?"

Jackson took a few steps toward her and she backed up a bit. She'd said too much too soon.

"I had you followed," she said defiantly.

Jackson moved closer. She retreated behind the bar. At least she got his attention. Any attention is better than none, she thought.

"You had *me* followed?" he yelled, pointing into his chest. He tried to contain his anger. She wasn't worth it.

"Yeah!" she spat. "I did! Then you know what else I did, Jackson?" she taunted.

He just stared blankly.

"I slept with Craig!" she screamed. "You know, the sheriff?" She started to pour herself a drink.

Jackson felt his head pulsating.

"And he was a good lay!" she continued. "That man can have you walking funny," she laughed. "Yeah, I felt like a new woman!"

Jackson was getting dizzy. He watched her throw back her drink and pour another. Then he turned to the door.

"Yeah, you do that!" she blasted. "You go scurry off to your little room, like you do every night. I don't need you!" She continued yelling as he disappeared through the door.

The dizziness was getting worse and a headache had begun. He'd just made it to the bedroom door, when he felt as if he was going to pass out. He opened the door and looked into the room. It was dark. He felt the wall for the light switch, but he unexpectedly dropped to the floor. He'd passed out and the recurring dream came flooding into his mind. It was much more clear this time...

He'd just returned from a business trip and stopped by to see George. He was re-writing his will. He decided he wasn't going to leave Darlene anything. He knew about her infidelities and even felt she and Kevin were seeing each other. Kevin was never a friend to him anyway. He was Darlene's 'childhood friend'.

Jackson was scheduled to leave immediately on another trip, but the flight was postponed for several hours. It had been a long, tiring day, so he decided to go in the morning. All he wanted now, was a hot bath, a beer and shot of whiskey to soothe his nerves.

Once home, he looked over the mail that was lying on the floor. He guessed he'd come home first. He went into his office and threw the letters on his desk. He would deal with them later. He walked up the stairs and down the hall to his bedroom. He paused for a moment. He thought he heard a noise.

He went close to door and listened. Yes, there was a noise coming from the other side. He placed his hand on knob and slowly turned it and pushed the door at the same time. The noise grew louder as the door widened.

It was dark. He could barely make out anything. He brushed his hand up the wall, searching for the light switch. Finding it, he clicked it on. He couldn't believe his eyes. Darlene was in bed with another man. It was his friend and attorney, George Davis.

"What the fuck is this?" Jackson roared.

George pulled out of Darlene and fell onto the bed. He scooted back quickly and grabbed the covers trying to shield himself from Jackson. Darlene covered herself with a sheet.

"Jackson, baby! Listen to me—" Darlene started.

He looked past her and to the man he had trusted all these years. "Shut up!" he boomed. "I don't want to hear your lying mouth. I know what you're about and I don't give a damn! But you, George! You!" Jackson balled his fists, then, becoming overwhelmed, he thought it best to leave immediately.

He stormed out of the house, slamming the door behind him. The force shook the foundation of the huge building. He fumbled for the keys in his pocket as his feet hit the pavement. He was so angry he could hardly push the unlock button on the remote for the car. He finally got in, started the engine and peeled away from the estate. "Damned woman!" he growled.

He broke every traffic law that had ever been passed. He just kept driving, far away… he didn't care where he ended up. The evening played in his mind over and over. "This is it! I can't take it anymore!" He yelled as loud as his voice could go. Eventually, he was speeding down an old country road. He was oblivious to the world outside. His mind wasn't straight. He kept thinking about the events of the day. He had no idea how long he'd been driving or where he was.

But suddenly, a deer ran into his path. He swerved to miss it and slammed on the brakes which caused him to slide from side to side, then veer hard toward a tree. Pain shot through his body and everything went black....

Slowly, Jackson awoke from his dream. He laid motionless on the floor. The recollection of that night filled his head. From start to finish, he remembered everything.

## Chapter 14

Jackson Marrell woke from a good night's sleep. He woke feeling much different than he had in a very long time, for this was the first morning in many months that he had complete recollection of who he was. He gazed around the room, comfortable with everything. And he knew this had been his room for over a year before his accident.

He sat on the edge of the bed, resting his feet on the plush carpet. He worked out a plan to teach both his wife and so-called friend a good lesson. Then another memory filled his mind. Dale. He couldn't forget her or what she'd come to mean to him. His heart still desired her, greatly.

Jackson took a cleansing shower, washing away the old and feeling refreshed with the new. Afterward, he took a long look in the mirror. Yes, he was back. And it felt great. A new day had come at last.

Every step he made, confirmed his memory loss was a thing of the past. He moved around his room with ease, knowing where everything belonged. And he knew the location of a few hidden things that only was aware of, like a stash of money he'd put back for a rainy day. He moved through the halls of the house looking at everything and knowing when and why he'd bought them.

He made his way down the stairs, whistling a tune he hadn't thought of in ages. He entered the kitchen area and went straight to the breakfast table. It was something he used to do.

The cook looked his way when she'd heard the cheerful whistling and was very surprised. "Mr. Marrell? You're eating in here?" she asked.

Jackson sat down and opened the newspaper. He raised his eyes to see the stunned expression on her face. "Yes, Glenda, I am," he said, giving her the same smile he used to. Then his eyes went back to the paper.

She quickly picked up some platters of food and brought them over. She placed them on the table, unable to take her eyes off of him. He laid the paper down and began serving himself. Glenda slowly walked away, scratching her head.

"Glenda," said Jackson. "I remember that I use to eat in here for breakfast. Before my memory loss. But that's over. I'm back—and with a vengeance!" he exclaimed.

"Good, Mr. Marrell! It's so good to have you back!" Her face lit up. He was definitely back. She went back to the counter to tidy up and to maintain a ringside view for whatever would unfold next.

Darlene had heard him get up and decided to come down to get on his nerves before he left for the restaurant. She headed for the dining room, where he'd been having his meals since his return, but he wasn't there. So she went to the kitchen to ask Glenda if she's seen him. When she walked through the door, she came to a screeching halt. She couldn't believe what she was seeing.

Glenda peeked around the corner and smiled wide. Yes, this was going to be a good day.

Jackson knew Darlene had come in, but did not acknowledge her. She glided over to the table where he continued eating and reading the morning news.

"Jackson?" she said.

He lowered the paper slightly and peered over the edge.

"Yes, Darlene?" he replied. He then folded the paper and placed it down to finish breakfast.

"You're eating in here?" she asked.

He sipped his glass of orange juice, then sat it down. Then his eyes went up to take her in. "Yeah, and?"

She stared back blankly and sat down as he went back to eating his food. She was hesitant to reply to that question.

He looked over to Glenda, who was still keeping a close eye, and gave her a thumbs up like he used to when she prepared his meals. Glenda smiled back, acknowledging him, and thankful he had regained his memory. She then left the kitchen to start her other duties, and to find the gardener. He needed to know the good news.

"You just gave Glenda the thumbs up," said Darlene, whose eyes were getting larger by the moment.

Jackson stopped eating for a second, glared at her, then shoved a half-eaten toast into his mouth. He washed it down with more juice. "You are so observant of things this morning, Darlene. Is there something you want to ask?"

She took in a deep breath then slowly let it out. "Is there anything you want to tell me?" she replied.

"Nope!" he said between bites.

She shifted in her chair. She was tired of being afraid his memory might be back. She couldn't stand the anxiety. "Okay, have it your way, Jackson. Do you remember anything?" she finally asked.

He took the last bite of food, not looking at her and swallowed it. "I remember a lot of things," he said. "Is there any particular memory you want to discuss with me?" He began to wipe his mouth with his napkin and looked sternly at her.

She bit her lips. His eyes told her what she wanted to know. They were strong and determined, not wide-eyed and innocent like they'd been the day before. "Your memory is back, isn't it?" she asked sharply.

He folded his arms and rested them on the table, leaning in to look dead into her eyes. "I remember enough," he said. "Like the night I left here so angry I wrapped my car around a tree and lost my memory."

Darlene was frozen.

"That night, I was supposed to go on a trip, but since the flight was delayed, I came home to get some rest. George knew about the trip, but he didn't know about the delay. So what does my trusted friend do? He came over here and banged my wife. That's what I walked in on, and that's what I tried to block out of my head. Until your confession of yet another banging, with the town sheriff, I didn't remember a thing."

He rose from his seat and began to pace back and forth. She felt her body trembling.

"Jackson, let me explain!" She left her chair and stood a distance from him.

"No!" he yelled.

She looked at him blankly, as if he had knocked all thoughts out of her head.

But he took a seat, trying to calm his nerves. He feared what he might do to her. He leaned back with his arms crossed and began to stroke his goatee.

Darlene tried to slow her breath, her heart was pounding hard against her chest. He'd divorce her, she thought. She began to panic. She couldn't stand the idea of losing all of this. She didn't care about him. It was the lifestyle she couldn't live without. What would she do? Then she thought of Dale. She would be the deciding factor in all of this. She gathered her courage. She couldn't let him have the upper hand. She reclaimed her seat and glared long and hard at him. "Does your memory include that other woman?" she asked boldly.

He lowered his head to glare back. "If you mean Dale, as a matter of fact, it does."

She stiffened, trying to keep her composure. She had to stay calm to win this round. "And what exactly do you plan to do, Jackson?"

"Whatever I damned-well please!" he replied. "You were the adulteress. So unless you want it to get ugly, don't fight me on this."

Her eyes grew dark with anger. "You son-of-a-bitch," she spat. "You listen to me and you listen good. I don't care how ugly this gets. But you should. After I tell my story of you leaving for all those months and shacking up with that woman, we'll see who gets dragged through the mud. She won't be able to show her face anywhere."

He didn't want Dale hurt, no matter what. "No my dear," said Jackson, "they will hear that I caught my wife and friend having sex in my bed which caused me an accident and a brain injury. Then how a brave woman risked her life to save me, and, at my request and fearing that there was a danger to my life, kept me safe."

He left his chair and began to relay to her the scenario of how convinced the court would be of who was the victim and who wasn't.

"You think you've got it all figured out, don't you?" she asked.

"Yes," he replied. "And you can't prove that she slept with me."

She rose from her chair and came to face him off. "Oh, but I can," she informed him. "A DNA test should do it." She then poured herself a glass of water. She was going to enjoy lowering the boom on him.

"DNA? Don't make me laugh," said Jackson. "I'm pretty sure there's no DNA left to find."

She leaned against the kitchen door and took a sip of water, smiling. "No, that's where you're wrong, Jackson. So much has developed since the last time you saw her. And in say… six months or so, DNA from that can give me the proof I need."

Jackson became still. "What the hell are you talking about?"

"Oh, didn't you know?" She covered her mouth and started to giggle. But he wasn't laughing.

"Don't play with me, Darlene! I've had it up to my throat with your antics," he warned.

She sat the glass down and slowly walked over to him. She wanted to get an up-close view, of the expression on his face when she told him the news. "Well, Jackson, yesterday I went to see your little girlfriend. You know, the one you hired a detective to find for you?"

Jackson's face muscles tensed. When he catches up with that weasel, he's going to wish he was never born. "You sabotaged my investigation? Typical!"

She smiled, knowing she now had the upper hand. "Don't you want to know what else?" she asked.

He put his hands on his hips and she could see it wasn't a good idea to prolong the torture much longer.

"Well, I figure since you let me know you went to see her, you're just dying to tell me what else," he said.

She sat down and crossed her legs. "I basically told her that you were looking for her. And that I wanted her to stay away from you."

"You little—"

She stood and raised her hands up to cut him off. "Wait, Jackson, there's more. You would have been proud of her. She told me to get the hell out of her house, and I knew she would have thrown me out."

Darlene went over to the window and stared out while she recalled the exact events. "I knew she meant it because as I was going to leave initially. The light from outside pierced the dress she wore. At first I thought she was a little thick around the middle, but then I saw it. A baby bump, round as can be. When I asked her about it, she became hysterical and yelled at me to leave. And you know me, I left as asked."

Jackson was silent. When Darlene turned around, he was slumped in a chair, unable to speak. A Cheshire grin stretched across her face.

The sword was drawn and driven, piercing the heart through. Darlene was contented knowing she had won this battle. There was nothing he could say or do. Basking in her victory, she turned to scowl at the man.

Jackson sat paralyzed from what he had just been told. Dale was having a baby–his baby, and she never told him. All these months, his one heart's desire had been her. She had given him the strength to go on and to see this thing through. All he wanted to was get his memory back so he would be complete and could start a new life with her. But now, it seems, she is no different than the she-devil standing before him.

"Are you sure she is having a baby?" he managed to ask. His voice was low and strained.

Darlene slithered over to her dejected husband. "Definitely," she said. "What's the matter, Jackson? Didn't she let you know she was pregnant? Oh, I know… maybe you forgot she told you."

Jackson jumped from his seat and quicker than lightning his hand was around her throat. She grabbed his hands trying to pry them away. She felt herself being pushed against the wall and lifted off the floor. Her back was pressing hard into it and her legs dangled in the air.

"I have done nothing but give to you," Jackson growled through gritted teeth. "And all you have done is take and take and take! And now you have managed to rip away the one thing I had to give me some ray of hope out of this hell. I have nothing left to lose. You may have won this round, but I will win the war. The gloves are off. You've been warned."

His voice was deep and his body trembled with rage. She could feel his hand tightening around her throat as she gasped for breath. Perhaps she'd gone too far this time.

He released her. She fell to the floor with a thud. Her hands immediately flew to her throat as she tried desperately to fill her lungs with air. She watched through a daze as he turned and walked away. This won't be good, she thought to herself.

Dale rocked back and forth in her chair, waiting for a call or an appearance. She didn't know what was going to happen next. But she knew Darlene couldn't wait to get home and tell Jackson that she was pregnant with his child. No one knew but Craig. He had come by, just in time to see Darlene leave. Dale told him of their confrontation and of her fears Darlene would tell Jackson.

Now he will feel she betrayed him too, but that wasn't the case. She did it to protect him and the baby. She didn't care what people said. She would have been the topic for a while until something worse came along to wag their tongues. She just felt it would be better for Jackson to get back to his life with no strings attached. He didn't need to be torn between his marriage and her and the child.

It had been a night of many that shouldn't have happened. Heck, he didn't even want to do it at first, because he was uncertain of their future. But she wanted him and didn't care about anything else. Only for that he complied. He shouldn't have to pay the consequences. He didn't know who he was or where he was from. She was fully in grasp of her right mind. Yes, this was her mess and she had to clean it up. For her unborn child and for Jackson. They deserved to be happy.

Darlene had managed to pull herself off the floor and crawl over to the table. She lifted herself into a chair. She slumped over on the table, her breath slow and her heart beating rapidly. She had never seen him this angry. This paled in comparison to the night he discovered her in bed with George.

In the years of their marriage, he had never raised a hand to her. No matter what she had done to piss him off. This thing ran deep. She had to warn both George and Kevin that Jackson's way was a good place to stay out of. Her head shot up when she heard the doorbell. She could hear Glenda talking to someone. It was a man. Good. Maybe it's George or Kevin. Saves her the task of contacting them.

"Mrs. Marrell, someone to see you," said Glenda. Darlene froze when she saw him. It was Craig. Glenda picked up on the reaction and waited to be dismissed.

## Chapter 15

Darlene finally came to her senses and waived Glenda away. Glenda was well aware of her mistress's extra-marital affairs. She figured this could be one of them. She huffed and went away.

"Sheriff, what are you doing here?" asked Darlene.

"That's the same thing I told you, when you showed up uninvited," Craig reminded her. "It seems that's somethin' you're good at." His words were short, and she could see that this wasn't a social call.

"Oh, I see that woman couldn't wait to tell you I came by," she said, rubbing her throat.

Craig took a seat even though he wasn't offered one. "No, I was driving up and saw you leavin'," he said. "She doesn't know I'm here. This is my doin'."

"Oh, I see," said Darlene. "Should I be afraid? After all, I've already been attacked once this morning." She removed her hands from her throat, revealing marks that were quickly turning black and blue.

Craig stared hard and long. "Your husband did that?" he asked, feeling his blood boil. One thing he had never been able to stomach was a man harming a woman—no matter what the case.

Inadvertently, Darlene had found a golden opportunity to salvage the battle. This will assure, Jackson will never be with Dale or the baby.

"Yes," she said, bringing up tears as a special effect.

Craig blew out a long hard breath. "What happened?" he asked.

Darlene pretended to have to gather herself together. "I told him about us," she said.

"What'd you go and do that for?" Craig said with surprise.

"He didn't know about the baby, so I told him. He was thinking about going after Dale, and I got angry." She covered her face with her hands then peeked through her fingers to see his reaction.

"Well, that ain't no way to treat a lady!" Craig exclaimed. "Or in your case, any woman."

She snatched her hands from her face furiously and glared at him. He just shrugged.

"You don't know how angry he can get," she said, getting back on topic.

Craig was still stunned. "This is weird," he said. "Jackson seemed like a pretty nice enough fella to me." Craig prided himself on knowing people. This one had him baffled.

"Yeah, that's the side of him you knew. But he has his memory back," said Darlene, getting comfortable in her chair.

"So he remembers everything?" said Craig. "Does he remember why he got into that accident in the first place? I'll need to finish my report."

"Yes," said Darlene. "But I wouldn't try to get it out of him right now. He's a little off today. You know what I mean?" She pointed to her throat.

"You should make a police report," said Craig. "He shouldn't be able to get away with that."

"What about Dale and the baby? He could go after her and I wouldn't want that on my conscience,"

Darlene lied. She cast her eyes downward, cradling her head in her hand.

"Don't you worry about Dale and her baby," said Craig. "I won't let him within ten feet of 'em." He then rose from his chair and walked out with a purpose.

Darlene watched him leave and a smile spread across her face, even larger than before. Mission accomplished. Jackson was never a challenge for her.

Jackson sat behind the desk of his business office. He was making plans that would have a great impact on his so-called loved ones. He was just setting aside some paperwork when a knock came at his door.

"I thought I told you not to disturb me unless it was an emergency," he said with a raised voice.

But when the person simply walked in, he was very surprised. It was Craig.

"What do you want?" asked Jackson, standing from his seat.

Craig stood firm. He wasn't going to let Jackson bully him. He came to make things plain. He wanted to tell him that Dale and the baby were off limits to him. "I came to talk to you man to man, if that's possible," said Craig.

Jackson offered him a chair. He was very curious as to why he'd come to see him. "Go ahead," he said before sitting back down.

"I went by to see you at your house," said Craig. "Saw your wife instead. I saw what you did to her. And she told me why you did it."

Jackson sat motionless, with no signs of emotions. "Get to the point," he said. "What is it you want to talk man to man about. Banging my wife?"

Craig swallowed hard. "Okay, I admit that wasn't a good idea," he said.

Jackson took a calming breath.

"Darlene came to the cabin lookin' for Dale," said Craig. "She said she had you followed and thought you'd seen Dale. She was so broken up about your rejectin' her, just like I was about Dale rejectin' me. We just got caught up in the moment.

Jackson's head turned slightly when he mentioned Dale rejecting him. "What were you doing at Dale's anyway?" Jackson asked.

Craig took in a breath and let it out. "I'm the one who bought the cabin from her."

"Do you know where she is?" asked Jackson.

Craig's back stiffened. "Yeah I know... but I'm not tellin' you," said Craig.

Jackson leaned back in his chair, staring daggers at Craig. "I didn't ask, now did I? I just asked if you knew where she was," Jackson said calmly.

Craig blurted out what he really wanted to say. "Well, seein' the type of person you really are, I think it's best for all if you keep your distance from Dale and the baby."

Jackson's voice grew deeper. "You sleep with my wife, then tell me it's not good for me to see Dale or my baby? Get it? My baby, not yours!"

"And it's Dale's baby too!" Craig exclaimed. "She has rights!"

Jackson eyes softened. "Does she know what she's having?" Jackson's voice was almost a whisper.

Craig's eyes narrowed. This was the man he knew from the cabin.

Jackson rose from his seat and walked around the room, thinking.

"No, she wants to be surprised," said Craig. "But I know."

Jackson looked at him.

"Would you like to know?" asked Craig.

"Yes," Jackson said sadly.

Craig could now see the battle Jackson was going through. "You're having a son," he said.

Jackson walked over to the window. "I won't bother Dale, or make trouble for her about the child. She's made it clear she doesn't want to have anything to do with me." Jackson felt the tears stinging his eyes. He was breaking.

Craig listened carefully and figured something was wrong with this picture. "Your wife–" he began, "she has bruises around her throat. Did you do that to her?"

Jackson continued to stare through the window. "I grabbed her and may have put too much pressure. I regret that. In all my years I have never raised my hands to a woman. And never will again. Darlene is the type of woman who will drive you to do many things. Lord knows she did this morning. It was my memory flooding my mind after she taunted me with the fact she had slept with yet another man. You."

Jackson sent this impact home well. Craig's mouth flew open and he realized something about the night he'd spent with Darlene. He hadn't been a comfort zone for, he'd been another victim. "Jackson, what happened that night?" he asked.

"I came home unexpectedly," he answered.

Craig got the idea. "She was with someone… that's why you fled. It was a friend, wasn't it?"

"Yes, a good friend," said Jackson. "That's why it had so much impact on me." Jackson was thinking of his beautiful son he will never be able to see or hold and of the woman who held his heart.

Craig stood silently. This was a horse of a different color. The man was in a den of thieves. They stole his love and dignity. Of course he would think Dale had done the same. "I'm sorry to hear that, Jackson. I knew you couldn't have been the monster she made you out to be."

Craig spoke to deaf ears. Jackson couldn't get past the fact that he was going to have a son—a son he would never see or hold in his arms. "If you're finished, I would like to be alone now. Let Dale know I won't be coming around to bother her."

Jackson's voice had a strange tone to it. Craig started to say something then thought better of it. He knew something of what Jackson was going through. He had felt that same thing, wanting something you can't have. But things were a little different with Jackson. He had something and lost it, so the pain was much greater. You can't miss what you never had, but to have it and lose it… well, that was something completely different.

Craig turned away and walked to the door. When he looked back at the man staring out the window, he felt for him. Leaving the office and closing the door behind him, he made a decision. One that was selfless.

## Chapter 16

Dale paced back and forth wringing her hands. Had she made the right choice? Did Jackson deserve to be kept from his child? No, he really didn't. He had been so loving to her. But he was married and deserved the chance to make it work. Knowing about the baby would hinder that.

She decided she was right and sat back in her chair. This was a mess.

Then the doorbell rang. She was relieved to see that it was Craig. She hugged him tight.

Craig was surprised at the greeting and returned the affection. "Hiya, Dale. What's goin' on?"

Dale closed the door behind them and leaned against it. Craig took a seat. He could see from the expression on her face that she'd been worrying.

"Come sit, Dale. We have a lot to talk about," he said.

She did as asked, but was confused and fearful of what he was going to say. "What is it, Craig?"

"I saw Jackson," he blurted.

Dale was stunned. "What?" she said.

"He won't be coming for you or the baby," said Craig. "Told me so himself. Gonna let your decision stand."

Craig watched for her reaction as he spoke. He wanted to know if she still loved Jackson before he told her the whole story.

Dale got up and walked away. "He knows about the baby?" she asked.

"Yeah, he knows," Craig confirmed.

"How?" she asked. She had to know if it came from Darlene.

"His wife told him." Craig wasn't giving too much detail, he needed to know her feelings, and he was starting to picking up on them.

"His memory is back, isn't it?" said Dale. There was a hint of sadness in her voice.

"Yeah," Craig replied. "He said it came back last night." When Dale turned back toward Craig, her eyes told him everything he needed to know.

"I need to confess somethin'," he said, "please sit down. It's been eatin' at me, since it happened."

Craig looked concerned. Dale took notice of this and came to his side. "What is it, Craig? You look so serious."

"I'm so ashamed. And since you're my friend, I have to tell you. Don't be my judge, just a friend," he pleaded.

"Of course, Craig. How can I judge you? Look at what I've done. And you have been nothing but supportive."

"Okay," he said. "Three months ago, I slept with a married woman."

Craig said it quickly and Dale's jaw dropped. Craig could hardly keep a straight face.

"Craig, you what? Who?" she asked, leaning forward.

"Jackson's wife." He just let it out and watched Dale's expression change.

Dale couldn't believe what just went through her ears. "You what?" she blurted loudly.

She jumped up and Craig followed suit. "Simmer down now, Dale. Let me explain."

She walked away, crossing her arms over her chest. "How could you be so stupid?" she scolded. Then she thought about her own situation.

"She seduced me," Craig admitted. "I couldn't resist."

Dale reclaimed her seat. She was beginning to dislike this woman even more. She has a beautiful man like Jackson and now she sleeps with Craig, Dale's best friend in the whole world. "Tell me what happened," she said.

Craig explained what had happened, just the way he'd explained it to Jackson.

"She came to the cabin, for me?" said Dale. "I'm not surprised. "And she surely lied about Jackson looking for me. If he was, why didn't he come here?"

Craig shrugged his shoulders. "I don' know," he said. "Darlene started talkin' about how Jackson wanted you and not her."

"But Jackson doesn't want me," she said. "Darlene should have kept those legs closed, and you my friend should know better. What were you thinking?"

"She reminded me of how much you wanted Jackson and that neither of you wanted us," Craig confessed. "She said she needed consolin' and so did I," he said sadly.

This was the hardest part. He still loved Dale, but now he knew for sure that she would always love Jackson. Dale's loss this time was different from when she's lost Thad. He had died and she had some type of closure. But Jackson was alive. He would always be a living ghost in her life.

Dale felt for Craig and everything he'd been going through. "I'm sorry, Craig," she said.

He stroked her face and gazed into her beautiful eyes. Now that he had her undivided attention, he would tell her the rest. She had to know everything before she made the biggest mistake of her life. That man loved her. So much so, he wasn't going to pursue seeing his son because Dale wanted it that way. Jackson believed that, but Craig knew better.

"This morning I went to Jackson's house, but he wasn't there," said Craig, "Darlene was. They'd been in a fight and she had bruises on her neck."

Shocked, Dale put her hand to her throat.

"Did Jackson do that?" asked Dale, afraid of the answer. The Jackson she knew would never touch a woman in that way.

"She'd provoked him, Dale," Craig insisted. "The woman is vicious. She told him the night before that we'd slept together. That's when his memory came back." Craig grew silent, letting that absorb into Dale's mind.

"What kind of monster is she? Dale said aloud. "I knew she was evil, but not like that." Tears stung her eyes. She felt so sorry for Jackson.

Craig continued. "Then this mornin', when she discovered he had his memory back—and knowin' he planned on comin' to you—she told him about your pregnancy. She teased him about the fact that you were having his child and hadn't told him. That was the blow."

Craig watched as the tears spilled over from Dale's eyes and flowed down her face. She sat there frozen in silence. His heart went out to her. He knew she was crushed from hurting this man who had decided to come straight to her after regaining his memory. He was coming to be with her and their child after all.

"So that you get the whole picture," said Craig, "the man didn't just lose his memory. He blocked out a bad one. He'd found his friend and his wife in bed together. And his friend and I were only part of a long list of affairs. That's why he was on the road that night. That's what led to the crash that led him to you. He was finally running away from the lies and the pain. But he came face to face with an angel... the one who would save him. If only you would."

Craig rose from the chair and placed a kiss on Dale's forehead. Before leaving, he gave one last backwards glance at the woman he loved. It was time for him to leave things in the past and reach out for the future. There was another wonderful woman who'd been after him for some time. It was high time he let her catch him and settle down. He hoped his friend would do the same.

## Chapter 17

Darlene looked in the mirror at the markings on her throat. She was surprised that he had so much fire, and she smiled when she thought about getting him into bed to show her some more. But the doorbell rang. She called for Glenda to answer, but remembered she'd sent her on an errand. She ambled to the door and swung it open. She froze in shock to see the woman on the other side.

"What the hell do you want?" she yelled.

Dale didn't say one word. She drew back her fist as far as she could and let it go. The impact was harsh. Darlene flew backward and smacked into the wall. Then she slid down coming to rest on the fancy tile floor. She covered her face with her hand and stared up at Dale, trying to gather her senses.

"That was for Jackson and my dear friend Craig," said Dale. "But the pleasure was for me! Come near any one of us again and you'll get much worse than that." Then Dale reached in and slammed the door.

Jackson sat at his desk lost in his thoughts. He'd been pining after a woman he thought loved him. The time they spent together fooled him. The things she had done to his body… and now that he could remember, no other woman has ever made him feel the way she did. He felt himself becoming aroused as he remembered those nights. Having given up on love, he would just have to go find some piece of tail to satisfy him later.

Then there was a commotion outside of his door. He had given strict orders not to be disturbed. And if they valued their lives, they wouldn't. But suddenly the door flew open.

"What the hell!" he yelled. The intrusion had so caught him off guard. That he lost his balance while trying to stand and fell backward out of his chair.

He laid there for a moment when he heard footsteps rushing his direction. He looked up to see the pair of legs come around the corner of the desk and stop. His eyes slowly traveled up them to the wide, curvy hips and slender waist, then to the full, rounded breasts. Ask and you shall receive, he thought. Then his mind registered something and his heart began to beat fast. He knew these body parts all too well.

Jackson looked down at the floor, thinking he was dreaming. He braced himself and attempted to lift himself up. The woman came over and began to help. When he got to his knees, she knelt down to meet him. And his eyes came to rest on the beautiful hazel eyes he'd woken up to on the morning after the accident. He stared into them as if he was dreaming.

"Jackson, forgive me for being such a fool all these months," she said.

He didn't know what to say. He didn't yet know exactly what she wanted from him. Had she come for reassurance that he would leave her and the unborn child alone?

"You didn't have to come," he said. "I told Craig I wouldn't come after you or the baby."

"I know what you told Craig," said Dale. "I know everything. I thought if you knew about the baby it would cause you problems in your marriage. It

177

was never because I didn't want you, Jackson! You have to know that."

Jackson felt for sure he was dreaming. He reached out and caressed her face with his hand. "Dale—is it really you?" he asked.

She looked into those gorgeous green eyes. "Yes, honey, it's me!" she replied.

Jackson stood to his feet. "You haven't changed since the last time we saw each other," he said.

"No," she agreed, "But sadly, you have, and it's partly my fault. I should have trusted you, Jackson, with everything. Memory loss or no memory loss."

Her voice was soothing. "Craig told you, huh?"

"Yes," she said. "He told me everything. I failed you, Jackson. I thought I was doing the right thing by letting you go and by keeping the pregnancy from you, but I'm here to correct that mistake."

"Are you sure that's what you want?" asked Jackson.

"Yes," she said. "I want you to be in my life–in our baby's life."

Dale felt her heart sinking. He was taking too long to respond. Maybe after all of this, he didn't want her anymore. Or worse, he didn't love her.

But Jackson couldn't take his eyes off of Dale. "Do you love me?" he asked, his eyes searching hers.

When she stared back at him, he knew.

"It seems you're always coming to my rescue," he said.

He pulled her onto his lap and kissed her. It had been too long since they had touched each other. They'd both longed for the day they could once again hold each other in their arms. He broke the kiss and his lips brushed against hers. She felt his warm breath on her lips she wanted more of him.

"Let's go, before we take this too far right here," he whispered.

"Oh!" she gasped and grabbed her midsection.

Jackson was confused. "What is it, Dale?" He could see she was in pain, but then her expression softened.

"I don't know. It was a—" she didn't finish as pain struck her again. "Jackson, I think I'm in labor… it can't be…it's too soon!" She started to cry.

Jackson laid her on the sofa and yelled for an employee to call an ambulance.

"No Jackson, it will take too long," Dale pleaded.

He understood what she was saying. He lifted her into his arms and carried her quickly to his car.

He laid her in the back seat and drove almost as fast as the night of the accident. But this time he was in complete control.

He made it to the hospital in record time. One of his cooks had called ahead, so the hospital staff was ready for them to arrive. They immediately took her to a room while Jackson paced back and forth waiting for news.

Finally, a doctor came out to see him. Jackson's heartbeat increased as he approached. He tried not to anticipate the worst. Maybe she shouldn't have made that trip to see him. Maybe he should have gone to her despite what he'd told Craig, then she would be safe at home.

"Are you the husband?" he asked.

"No," said Jackson. "But I am the father." It felt good to say he was the father. "How are they?" he asked, anxiously.

"She had what we call false labor pains," said the doctor. "Mother and baby should be just fine, but I think she should stay off her feet for the remainder of the pregnancy."

Jackson breathed for the first time since they got there. "How long will she be here?" he asked. He didn't want her to have to stay there longer than

180

necessary. And he didn't want her to have to encounter Darlene.

"She can leave anytime she is ready," the doctor replied. "But she will need to have someone home with her at all times until the birth."

"She will," Jackson assured him. "Can I see her?"

"Yes, follow me."

Jackson had called Craig's office and let him know what happened. Dale was sleeping when Jackson came to her. He sat down in a chair and held her hand. He stayed that way until she awoke.

"Jackson," she said softly. "Let's go home."

He loved hearing those words. "Yeah, let's go home," he said and gave her a long, lingering kiss. When they left the hospital that day, their new life was just beginning and the troubles of the past were far behind.

Dale gave birth to their son at forty weeks on time. They named him Jack Dale Marrell. They lived happily ever after, for nothing and no one can stand in the way of what the heart truly desires.

For more information, visit the author's official website, www.SRBurks.com